Within A Week

Within A Week

Galen Rose

Copyright © 2020 by Galen Rose.

Library of Congress Control Number: 2020905392
ISBN: Hardcover 978-1-7960-9502-9
Softcover 978-1-7960-9501-2
eBook 978-1-7960-9500-5

All rights reserved. No part of this book may be reproduced or transmitted in any form or by any means, electronic or mechanical, including photocopying, recording, or by any information storage and retrieval system, without permission in writing from the copyright owner.

This is a work of fiction. Names, characters, places and incidents either are the product of the author's imagination or are used fictitiously, and any resemblance to any actual persons, living or dead, events, or locales is entirely coincidental.

Any people depicted in stock imagery provided by Getty Images are models, and such images are being used for illustrative purposes only.
Certain stock imagery © Getty Images.

Print information available on the last page.

Rev. date: 03/19/2020

To order additional copies of this book, contact:
Xlibris
1-888-795-4274
www.Xlibris.com
Orders@Xlibris.com
811252

WITHIN A WEEK

I'm barely conscious. I can feel the medical technicians pumping me with them damn electrode things. I don't really know what's going on with me but all I do know is that I can feel a lot of pain within my chest. I'm having a very difficult time breathing. Every inhale I take feels like my ribs can't withstand another breath. The ambulance that I'm in has just turned the corner onto Grider street. The sirens bellow loudly as I lose all consciousness.

    I don't know how long I've been in this realm of nothingness but when I do finally come too it feels like days have gone by. I'm guessing that one of these many IV's that's attached to my body will alert a nurse. My first thought was to pull one loose but at the slightest effort I was overcome with a sharp pain that caused me to cry out like a baby. No more than 10 seconds later a nurse rushed in to check on my wellbeing. The pain was so intense that I lost vision for a beat. As I steady my gaze and regain my focus I was happy to notice that my hormones and desire for women wasn't injured. The nurse that came into the room was fine as hell and she had a PHAT ass. She was facing me but I could easily see her flared hips just being pushed out by her juicy ass. My crying like a baby stopped promptly and my dick got hard enough to make the gown I was wearing cry!! I was hoping she didn't see my bulge; I don't think she did because the first thing out of her mouth was, "Good afternoon Mr. Chambers, how are you feeling? Can I get you anything to drink?"

I tried to reply but my mouth was so dry that no words escaped my lips. All I was able to do was nod my head. She put a straw to my dry lips and I winced from the pain that shot through my body as I tried to raise my head. She noticed my pain and told me to let her do all the work and I'm to just pull on the straw. After the water gave my voice some life I said, "I'm not feeling too good right now. My chest hurts like hell and it's difficult to breathe due to the pain in my chest."

"Don't worry, I'll turn up your medication to reduce the pain." She reached over and opened a valve on one of the IV bags to allow a more steady flow of drugs to attack my body. As she was doing that she smiled at me and said, "My name is Nakesha I'll be your nurse for the next several hours. Anything you may need or want, I'll be here for you. Can you eat Mr. Chambers? Your medication takes effect in a short while."

I struggled to get the question out but I managed, "Nurse Nakesha, what happened to me? Why am I here?" She looked at me with a shocked expression and asked if I was serious. I told her that I was very serious. She then told me to tell her what I do remember.

CHAPTER 1

"Say fool, run into the store and grab 2 green dutches and 2 Vitamin waters," I said to my lil homie Sleaze. We were on our way to scoop up these 2 fine ass Monkeys to fuck off with.

As Sleaze got out of my get'm mobile I decided to run over to the pay phone to call my Monkey to let her know to have her friend ready cause we'll be there in 20 minutes.

Before any of you readers getting to thinking stupid, I have 3 cell phones. One for my licks, another for my family and the other for my plug. I don't use any of my phones to call any Monkeys. As I snatched the phone from the cradle a car came around the corner at a high rate of speed that caused the driver to lose control. The tires were screeching trying to gain traction. I could see the driver's eyes as he realized that the car was doing its own thing and he was just going along for the ride. Before I knew it the car was heading directly at me and the pay phone. It seemed like my only options was to get plastered into the wall with the pay phone or use my God's given athletic skills and let the phone drop from my hand and attempt to jump onto the car. Without question I chose to become a hurdler and jump onto the car. I was damn near successful in clearing the whole car completely but my feet got clipped by the top of the windshield. It was exactly what caused me to lose balance and sent me crashing chest first onto the top of the car. I lost all my air and I blacked out off and on until I was fully aware of Nurse Nakesha's fine ass. After

I gathered my wits and thoughts, I told her everything that I just told you.

"Well yes Mr. Chambers, you were in an accident involving a car 2 days ago. The doctors thought that you've suffered internal damage due to the extensive outlook of the situation. Luckily you've only suffered several fractured and cracked ribs. Do you have pain anywhere else?" Asked Nurse Nakesha.

"Nah Beautiful, I'm cool everywhere else but my chest."

"We've taken X-Rays and they hadn't revealed any other damage. I can see that one of your organs is working very well and is in tip top condition," she said as she eyed my hard-on. I just grinned at her and smiled my bitch-getter smile. I'm assuming that my smile did it because she made it her business to rub her PHAT ass against my hand. Out of the blue my room door opened up and my lil homie Sleaze came in saying, "Damn playboy, it's about time that you woke up. It's been 2 whole days since we last saw each other dawg."

I smiled at my lil homie and my erection instantly deflated. I took the formal approach and introduced Sleaze to Nurse Nekesha. After introductions were made Nurse Nekesha exited the room and left me alone with this damn fool Sleaze. I gently turned to face him and said, "What up kid? How's shit going out there?"

"Man everything is everything. Since you've been layin up here I've been taking care of your business in the streets. That nigga Damage keep asking about you. I heard that he just came up on 20 bricks. I think that he wants to toss you a few. He gave me this number for you to hit him up," Sleaze said as he produced a piece of paper for me. "Oh yea, I got them 7 stacks from Ray-Ray and the 4 from Otis," Sleaze said as he gave me a paper bag filled with dead presidents. I stuffed the bag under my pillow without feeling any pain. It's crazy how that bread can make you ignore some pain. Pussy does that too somehow. Sleaze gave me his phone and I called Damage; he answered on the first ring, "who dis", he asked.

"What up Damage? This is Chips. You been looking for me?" I asked.

Within A Week

"Yea Chips, what's good my nigga? How are you holding up? Heard you almost found God in the wrong way, not the long way."

"Yeah my dude, shit was ugly but it's not that serious. I'm good. What's on ya mind? Kick it while I listen," I said.

"Is this a safe phone to kick it with you on?" He asked.

"No doubt. what's good?"

"I'm trying to fuck with you bruh. You already know I play the pistol game but my cousin just came here and he brought some work with him. I know that you stay knee deep in that game and I want to work something out with you."

"Work something like what out?" I asked him.

"If you buy 10 I'll front you 10."

"Sounds good so far. What's the number on the buy and front?"

"You can buy for 15 stacks each and the front gonna be 17", he said matter of factly.

I paused for a second just to make him think that I was weighing my options but I wasn't gonna let those numbers get pass me. "When will you be ready for me and when will you be expecting the front paper?"

"You can get it whenever you want. The front bread you can get to me next week. If you want, you can send ya man Sleaze to come get it if you still need time to heal or whatever."

I sat there quiet for a minute to contemplate my decision and then said, "Alright Damage, I'm gonna send Sleaze your way with the 150 stacks. He'll hit you up at this number and from this number when he's ready."

"Cool Chips, I'll holla at you later. Get right and stay up", Damage said as he hung up. I turned back to Sleaze and gave him his phone back. I looked him in his eyes and said, "I don't know what's going on but I'm down if you're down."

"You already know what it is with me, my dude. Just send me to him and I'll handle it."

"That's what's up my nigga. Make sure that you strap-up when you go see that nigga. You already know that he's a livewire hothead who bust his hammer."

"Chips that shit about him is old shit!!! What has he done lately?" Sleaze asked. My lil homie was going into this situation wrong, so I had to enlighten him and pull his coat to some facts. So I told him this, "Do you remember 2 weeks ago when Manny got hit up in a robbery?"

"Yea I remember. Damage did that?"

"Nah lil homie, Damage didn't do that. Manny was Damage's right hand back in highschool. Damage love that nigga like I love you."

"So why are you talking about that Manny shit?"

"Check this out Sleaze, Damage have been killin niggaz for about 10 years. He hasn't got caught because he's very calculating. Yea he's erratic at times. However, he's always dangerous. Not too many people know this but them 2 young boyz that got their heads knocked off 3 days ago on Genesee and Rother?"

"You're not talking about Gusto and Savage? Them 2 wild niggaz that was sticking up the town? The ones found in the 69 position?" Sleaze asked.

"Yea.... Them 2 niggaz. That was Damage work. Don't ask how I know. Just know that Damage is still putting niggaz dick in the dirt. Just pay attention while you're handling this business," I told my lil homie.

Sleaze had to remind me that he gets down for his. He said, "I'm good with my gun game big homie, you already know though. I'll be alert and paying attention. When do you wanna take care of it?"

"You can get to as soon as you leave here. before you go though hit me with some smoke so I can get my mind right."

CHAPTER 2

Chester is a long time dopehead who's been sniffing and shooting that BOY forever it seems like. After Sleaze left the hospital from seeing me Sleaze bumped into Chester at the store on French & Kehr. Chester saw the opportunity to come up with a few dollars and turned on what he thought was charm, "If it ain't my main man Sleaze!!! Help a player out. I got this desire weighing me down young player and I really need help lifting it up off me. Toss a dog a bone."

"Pops you need to check yo ass into the hospital and clean yo ass up. You are running around here looking and smelling dead. You're lucky you're Chips dad or I wouldn't do shit for your old sorry ass. He told me not to fuck with you so you better keep yo mouth shut about me looking out for you. Come to the spot on Hurlock in a half hour. You can clean the dog kennels and I'll give you a few dollars to lift that fucked up habit off you."

Sleaze ran into the store to get whatever he was getting and headed to Hurlock. When he got in the house he removed the pistol from his waist and chained the dogs in the yard. He went back into the house and rolled up a dutch while he waited for Chester. As he waited he called Damage to set up the exchange. As soon as Sleaze got off the phone Chester walked on the porch and went to knock but Sleaze was already there with a hammer in hand. He said to Chester, "I don't have all day. I have shit I gotta take care of, so do a good and quick job. I'll bless you when you're down."

"Alright young player I'll do a quick and good job for you", Chester beamed at Sleaze with lust off the idea of getting his fix.

While Chester was cleaning, Sleaze called me. I asked after I answered, "what up young gunner?"

"I was calling to let you know that I got that bread and I'm meeting dude when the sun goes down."

"Alright cool. Just be on point my dude. Call me when everything is taken care of and you put them bricks up."

"I got you Big homie. I'll hit you up later."

Before Sleaze hung up I heard my no-good dopehead father in the background. I heard him say to Sleaze, "I'm all done young player. You got something for me?" I yelled through the mouthpiece, "Sleaze what the fuck is he doing there? I thought I told you not to fuck with that nigga?"

"Chillout Chips. He came by because he heard what happened to you. Since he was here I figured it wouldn't hurt if I let him clean out the kennels. My bad for not listening but it was all in good faith."

"Alright lil bruh. Make sure you keep your eyes on his crooked ass and get him out of there sooner than later." Sleaze ended the call and gave Chester $25 to help him get his cravings taken care of and something to eat.

Chester rushed out of the house and headed in a beeline straight to the dope spot on Montana. He was skipping up the street like a little kid while whistling the tune from the Pink Panther cartoons. He was very oblivious to his surroundings as he walked right in front of a Frito Lay delivery truck that was pulling up to the store on Goodyear & Ferry. The truck wasn't going fast but it was going fast enough to hit Chester and toss his narrow ass several feet up the street. He landed hard and awkward to where he looked like a crumpled bag of chips. He wasn't moving and looked to be dead. An ambulance was called and showed up 10 minutes later. Chester was rushed to the hospital. Being that he did years of abuse to his body his pulse was very light. At the hospital the doctors took his blood for testing and X-Rays for broken bones. The X-Rays revealed a tear in his lungs where one of his ribs broke and punctured it. He was bleeding internally which caused the doctors to begin operating immediately. After opening Chester's chest up the doctors were able to see that Chester was deteriorating from the inside. All of his organs were being chewed away from the many years of heavy drug usage and cigarette smoke. His blood test came back to reveal that Chester had severe Cancer among other shit. The doctors figured Chester to be dead by this time next week. The doctors left Chester's chart on the end of his bed after the surgery. The charts determined that Chester has almost a week of life left. A nurse came for the chart and put all the information into the medical files in the computer.

CHAPTER 3

"Say Damage I'm here bruh. Where are you at?" Sleaze asked him over the phone.

"I'm pulling up in a minute."

Sleaze was inconspicuous as can be. He donned some regular workers overalls, a pair of beat up construction boots and he drove a beat up van with the shedding words "Joe's Maintenance". He was parked on a side street off of Bailey in front of an abandoned house. Three minutes later Damage and a nigga that Sleaze never seen before hopped out of a Honda Accord. They strolled up to Sleaze and Damage introduced the dude to him. "Sleaze what up? This my cousin Shellz. He'll be around for a min and you may have to deal with him on the business side of things in the future. I figured it would be cool for you to meet him now instead of later." Sleaze and Shellz slapped each other up like they knew each other for years. Sleaze turned to Damage and said, "you already know Chip's situation. He won't be home until tomorrow I believe. He'll wanna get up with both of y'all to familiarize himself with his cousin here. That's tomorrow but I got that bread for the situation right now."

"Word. That's what's up. I got those bricks in the car. You got that bread for the first half?"

"Facts. It's in the van."

Damage went to the car and came out with a duffle bag and hopped in the van with Sleaze. He said, "you already know that this game here isn't my game but I'm putting my name on it. Tell Chips he can step on them if he wants to".

"That's what's up," Sleaze said as he gave Damage the book bag that contained the bread. "Count it fair it's all there."

That slapped up and Damage hopped out of the van and got back in the Accord. Sleaze pulled off and made it to his destination and stashed the bricks. Then he called me. I was sitting up watching basketball while Nurse Nekesha was giving my body an alcohol rub. I answered saying, "talk about it."

It seemed like this nigga knew what was going on because he said, "what's good pimpin? How's the body feeling?"

"You already know my dude. I'm good. The good Nurse Nekesha is rubbing me down right now. I'm feeling brand new right now. How did everything go with that situation?"

"Everything went smoothly. I met his cousin Shellz during that meeting."

"Word? What breed of nigga did he appear to be?"

"He looked like he carried the same genes as Damage. I had the strap ready though."

"Another live-wire huh man?"

"Hell yeah, but the cousin has a laid back demeanor. I looked in his eyes and saw that he carried that Damage shit in him."

"Everything was correct with the work?"

"Yeah..... Everything is sweet. You're gonna love it."

"That's what's up," I said.

"I told Damage that you'll wanna get up with him and meet cousin yourself sooner than later."

"Cool, I'll be discharged in the A.M. So be up here to get me around 9 in the morning."

"I got you. Yo Chips, why didn't you ask me about your whip?"

"I didn't feel there was a need to ask about it. I trust you with my life so I know that you'll take care of my whip with the same care."

"You already know my nigga. I'll be there early. Want me to bring you some food up there later?"

"Nah. I'm good fool. See you in the A.M." I said as I hung up.

* * * * *

"So Mr. Chambers you know that you'll have to rest yourself when you're released tomorrow. No drinking, partying or anything that can cause a lot of strain on your body" nurse Nakeha stated.

I smiled my killer smile and said, "You don't have to worry about me drinking cause I don't drink and as for the partying goes, I am the party!! Can you tell if getting some neck will cause strain on my body?"

Nurse Nakesha outwardly blushed and strolled casually to the door and locked it. When she came back to my bed she snatched the sheet down and slid my hospital gown up near my chest and said in a seductive voice, "let's see if some crazy neck will put some strain on you!?" I knew my killer smile had its effect. Nurse Nekesha then took me into her warm mouth and blessed me with some crazy wild neck. Before long I was cumming in her grill. She treated my nutt like henny and swallowed me back. She released me and said, "I don't think getting neck should be a problem." She rose up and kissed me on the cheek and said, "you taste so good. I'm gonna put my number in your phone. I'm off for the next 3 days so I won't be here when you're discharged tomorrow. Call me ASAP so that we can get up and do some real freaking."

I smiled my smile and said, "You got it baby girl. Put those credentials in my horn and I'll definitely hit you up." Nurse Nekesha cleaned me up, brushed her teeth and left me until tomorrow.

* * * * *

Chester lay in excruciating agony as the doctor examined his ragged body. He can see that Chester is malnourished, sick and in his own opinion; repulsive. He wondered what had happened to this man that led him to such a horrendous state.

Within A Week

While he was being examined, Chester kept falling in and out of consciousness from all the pain he was experiencing. It wasn't just the accident that had him in so much pain. He was also hurting because he never did get his fix and his body kept reminding him of it. He was in a huge state of Dope Sickness. He had all kinds of tubes running through his mouth and nose that he was unable to speak. He so desperately wanted to tell the medical staff that he was a regular Heroin shooter. Several minutes later Chester got a brief bit of luck. A nurse came into his room and gave the doctor a clipboard and read from it. The information on the paper was from the Buffalo Police Department. It stated that Chester was a known petty criminal that had a severe addiction to Heroin and could possibly need a counter drug to help ease his pain. After reading that part the doctor said to him, "I think that I have something to help ease the other pain." He then ordered the nurse to set up an IV bag for Morphine use. After the IV was installed and Chester felt the first trickle of the drug his body began to relax and some of the pain eased away. It felt like his body was doing somersaults and applauding!!! Chester fell into a deep sleep that lasted forever!!

CHAPTER 4

"So cousin, what's the line on Sleaze and this Chips nigga?" Shellz asked his cousin Damage.

Damage replied, "Chips is a boss type nigga that have a few crackhouses spreaded throughout the town. He's very quiet, lowkey and about his business. He's very smart, careful, loyal and he's a real nigga at all times."

"I hear that. So that front money is in good hands then?"

"No doubt. That's why I chose him to deal with. Besides, He's known me for a long time. He knows how I give it up."

"What's the deal with Sleaze?" Shellz asked.

"His name says it all. He was a no good bum-ass nigga until Chips took him under his wing. Chips straightened him out and got him on some getting money shit. Chips still let the young nigga stay Sleazy at times. Sleaze really isn't a hustler or a stick-up nigga. He's just Chips right hand and dirt doer. Whoever crosses Chips, Sleaze will await for Chips to say so and quietly down him."

"So we should watch that nigga Sleaze close?" Asked Shellz.

"Nah cuz, them dudes are alright. If they weren't I would've offed them niggaz a long time ago. Chips could have paid for all 20 bricks if he wanted too. He's probably got a half mil stashed somewhere."

"Why did we front him then?"

"Because Chips don't know you. I'm not known for moving work and the best way to get a true nigga like Chips to trust us was to front

Within A Week

him. Besides, we get a little more bread out of the deal. He isn't going anywhere, the money is in good hands."

"Alright, it's your show", Shellz said as he lit up a dutch.

* * * * *

"Alright Shellz, tell me what happened back in Florida that made you bounce with them 20 bricks."

"Man, a couple of partners of mines- well they not really my partners but I knew both of them from fucking with a few bitches. Anyway, I was on the beach one night about to hit the club up when I ran into these niggaz outside. One of them; his name was Ty."

"Wait a minute. What do you mean by was?"

"Let me finish. Anyway, Ty and his boy Jay had some Cali buds to blow so we walked down to the shore of the beach and blew 2 blunts. Where we blew at was rumored to be a drop off spot for this Colombian dude. As we were about to leave I looked at the water and saw something floating near the surf. Then I heard a couple voices yell for us to get the fuck from over there. Then 2 clown ass Colombians ran up on us carrying mac 11's. The 2 niggaz I'm with, Ty and Jay had the idea that floating in the water was bricks and planned on getting them. When the Colombians came close enough Ty and Jay grabbed the guns and tussled with the Colombians. As the four of them were tussling I pulled out my hammer and got to nailing shit!! My first shot hit one of the Colombians in the throat and left him slumped on the sand. Ty then picked up the fallen mac and sprayed the other Colombian and his own man Jay!! When I saw that happen I became nervous and antsy. Ty then turned to me without compassion in his face. Something told me that he was about to open up on me so I beat him to it and tore his head off his shoulders!!"

"Damn cousin, that's some wild shit right there. What happen after you sent the nigga Ty to hell?" Asked Damage.

"So I'm standing inbetween 4 dead muthafuckaz and something still floating in the water. I started thinking that the reason the

Colombians reacted to us like they did and by the way Ty murked his boy Jay, the answer for all that carnage is floating in the water. So I went into the water and grabbed what turned out to be a water cooler. I carefully made my way to my whip without being noticed and went home. Once I got to the building I opened the cooler and pulled out the package that contained 20 bricks of that Colombian fire."

"Damn cuz, you got lucky with that come up."

"Nah cuz, not really."

"What? The hell you didn't. Why do you say that?"

"Because I'm in Buffalo by force."

"How do you figure? Why do you say that?"

"The damn Colombians were smart. They hid a small gps device in the cooler. I'm guessing that everything was a time set for the pick-up. After I removed the work I went to toss the cooler out and saw this fiend named Monty walking by so I just gave it to him. About 90 seconds later I heard some loud gibberish a few doors down and I went to my porch and looked to see what it was. My eyes bulged crazily when I saw Monty surrounded by 4 Colombians yelling incoherent words. I'm guessing that Monty must've understood what they were saying because Monty pointed towards my crib. Before his snitch finger was able to fall back by his side a lil Colombian bitch put the barrel of her sig to his head and I heard a burst of rounds before I saw the top of Monty's head fly in the air. Brain and blood sprayed into the air like you see in the movies cousin. There was no question in my mind that Monty had given them what they wanted; and that was my crib!! Seeing what they did to Monty only left me positive that I was gonna meet the same fate or worse if they got ahold of me."

"Damn fam, that sounds like some movie shit right there. Let me guess, you got the drop on them and sent them to hell?"

"Hell nah nigga!! I put the work in a duffel bag and slid out the back door into the alley and ran faster then that Jamaican nigga to my hooptie that I left stashed in my man garage. Before I was able to get 30 seconds away from there I heard hella gunfire as them muthafuckaz lit into my crib."

Damage was laughing as he said, "No shit!!! You're a wild boy. With yo scary ass. I would've downed 4 more Colombians."

"Man fuck that shit. Where the hoes at? I'm ready to fuck off on a few bitches."

"I got you cuz. C'mon let's go over by UB and fuck with some college hoes."

CHAPTER 5

I was just laying on the bed watching the 11 o'clock news thinking what I was going to do tomorrow when I get up out this bitch. I know for a fact that the very first thing I'm going to do is check on my crib and make sure that all is well there. Then I'm definitely going to get me some real food; probably GiGi's. Fuck it, I might just go to Matties. Wherever it is I'm getting right. Then I'll go to the stash spot and check out them 20 bricks. If them joints are correct I'll step on 10 of them and load my houses up. After that I'll hit Nurse Nekesha up and chill out with her for the rest of the day at the casino in the Falls. I don't even know why I'm telling y'all this because shit never goes the way we plan.

    As I come out of my thinking zone I can hear the newscaster saying, "there was an accident on the east side earlier today. An elder man was rushed to ECMC after being hit by a corner store delivery truck. Witnesses on the scene stated that the man-whose name isn't yet known-was oblivious to his surroundings and just walked out into the path of the delivery truck. Witnesses say that the collision wasn't as bad as the outcome, but my sources at the hospital tells that the unknown man has slipped into a coma. That's all that we have at this time; reporting from the channel 5 newsroom. I'm Rachel Howard reporting."

Within A Week

I was feeling elated for my release in the morning but that bit of news made me realize how lucky I am to be alive. I just had a similar type of situation and I barely got scratched. And this old head get hit like me and he's stuck in a coma. His life is virtually over. God bless that man's family.

CHAPTER 6

"My man Damage, how's it going?" Asked the bouncer of the strip club Extasy. Damage had decided to take his cousin Shellz there to see some stripper hoes. Pretty much everyone that worked there knew who Damage was by face. Some knew him personally. He was a regular there. Extasy was a fancy strip club that catered to the upscale men. It's also the place where Damage relaxes, chill and stake out his robbery victims. He wasn't just a straight up killer, although he has killed many, it just turned out to be the outcome of the situation. It wasn't known that he was a stick-up kid; that was mainly due to the fact that most of his victims never saw his face and the ones that did are resting in pieces.

At the club Damage has a loyal, honest and fully trustworthy Monkey who puts him on to the right people to rob. His Monkey name is Kandy. And boy was she sweet!! Kandy was the very essence of a Dime Piece. She was an ice cold redbone with unblemished features and a very smooth skin tone to match. She had almond shaped eyes and some full luscious lips that Damage loved to kiss on. She had a tiny nose and some long Auburn hair that went well with her skin complexion. Kandy also sported a knockout figure. Her measurements were respectively 38d-26-42. Her ass was so wide and Phat. She always looked delicious. Kandy was the black man's ideal and the white boyz fantasy. All it takes is one look and your lustful desires will rise and the money in your pockets will grow legs and run after her and into her g-string. At first glance you'd think you were looking at a thicker Mexican Meagan Goode.

Within A Week

"Hey what's up Rocky, everything good tonight?"

"Man, it's all good here. There's a few people inside and the women are always hot. Of course your favorite is here running things like she always does."

"Oh yeah? That's what's up. This here is my cousin Shellz Rock. Can you hook me up with my favorite spot in the back and have a bottle of Remy and a bottle of Patron sent to the table for me Rocky?"

"I got you bruh. Nice meeting you Shellz, enjoy yourself and have a good night."

"No doubt. Nice meeting you also," Shellz replied.

As they headed toward their table Shellz looked back and saw that Rocky had moved on and was using his wand on the next group of people entering the establishment. Shellz turned back to Damage and asked, "why didn't dude use that wand on us?"

"I'm known in the streets and I'm known here. I get VIP treatment here. I don't go through any of the regular regulations."

A sexy waitress came over to their table with the bottles they ordered and 4 glasses. She also handed Damage a pen and a piece of paper then said, "The DJ said to put down the tracks you wanna hear for the next hour." She then turned away and sashayed her sexy ass for all the men to see. Shellz said to Damage, "Damn cousin, who is this fine ass bitch coming our way?"

Damage smiled and said, "Chill cuz, that's my main bitch right there." Kandy strolled over with all her glamorous beauty on display. She was smiling and strutting her flawless attributes because she was able to see that the dude with her nigga was off balance due to her beauty. She walked up to Damage and planted a big kiss on his cheek and said, "Hi Daddy!! I've been missing you. Where has my King been?"

Damage smiled and said, "hey Gorgeous, I've missed you also. I've been handling business as usual. How have you been?"

"I've been fine. I'm doing so much better now that you're in here", Kandy said as she rubbed here juicy titties on his face. Damage got a quick flash of anger and said to her, "Bitch don't be trying to treat me like one of your Johns!! Don't be rubbing your titties on my face.

Sit your ass down." Just as his temper came it disappeared. He said, "This is my cousin Shellz. He's from Florida. He's gonna pick out one of those bitches he wants for the night and I want you to make sure that he gets her."

"I got you Daddy. Sorry for upsetting you. Hi Shellz, how are you and how do you like our city so far?"

"How are you doing ummm?"

"Kandy."

"Yes; Kandy. How are you?"

"I'm fine. Thank you for asking."

"That's good. Buff is pretty cool so far. There's a lot of beautiful women here. I just met the finest one of them all", Shellz said as he flirted with her at the same time giving an honest compliment.

"Thank you Shellz, that was very kind of you to say. If you'd like, I'd set you up with something really sweet for the night."

"That's cool. I'll leave everything in your hands."

Damage broke up the little conversation between Shellz and Kandy by saying to Kandy, "baby girl, pour 3 glasses of each for us. Take your drink with you and take this playlist to the DJ for me. Come back with someone to keep my cousin company while we go to the private room."

Kandy got up and did what she was told. While she was gone Damage said to Shellz, "cousin, I gotta go take care of something with this girl. If you see something you like go with your game. If you need to just tell her that you're here with me and Kandy. Drink as you will and I'll be back shortly."

As soon as Damage said what he had to say, he tossed back his Patron and chased it with Remy as he followed Kandy's Phat ass to a private room located further back in the establishment. He smiled all the way until the door closed behind him.

CHAPTER 7

"Hey handsome, what's good?" Asked the tall blond with the body of Ice T's wife CoCo.

Shellz wasn't paying attention until he looked up and saw that there were 2 girls not one. He spit up his drink and said, "Damn!! Excuse me spitting up but I'm not accustomed to being thrown off like that."

The 2 girls laughed and introduced themselves, "I'm Peaches and this is my twin sister Cream." They both smiled at him.

"What's up beautiful ladies? Y'all name definitely fit y'all to a tee. Y'all are some very beautiful women. Have a seat and have a drink with me. My name is Shellz." He signaled the waitress and asked for another pair of bottles and 2 more glasses as the twins took a seat. After the waitress left, Shellz poured the twins a drink and said to them, "please don't view me as being rude but what race are y'all?"

Simultaneously they said, "Italian and Caribbean."

"That's a helluva combination. Y'all are fine as fuck!! How old are y'all?"

Peaches spoke up and said, "we're 23 and 3 months. I'm older than Cream by three minutes flat. Our birthday is on different days though."

"Really? How is that?" Shallz asked a bit confused.

Cream smiled and said that her sister was born at 11:59 pm and she was born at 12:02 am.

"That's wild shit right there. I never heard anything like it. I must say again that y'all are a pair of gorgeous women."

Simultaneously again the twins said, "Thank you Shellz."

"So what are y'all doing working here instead of walking down a runway or modeling swimsuits or something like that?"

Peaches said, "we don't appeal to the traditional standard of modeling. We tried but we were told that we are too big for the recognized American modeling. Besides, we're only doing this to help pay for our schooling. We're both studying to become lawyers. We're in our third year right now. We'll receive our degrees sooner than later. Soon after that we'll be a step closer to achieving our goals."

That's what's up. I'm very impressed with y'all. You both are young, gorgeous and smart. Those are some deadly combinations. Especially with it being 2 of you."

Fifteen minutes later Damage and Kandy joined the trio. Damage told Kandy to excuse herself and the twins because he had to kick some things around with his cousin. Before Kandy left he pulled her to whisper in her ear. He told her to make sure that the twins spend the night at the condo tonight. He patted her on her juicy ass as she and the twins left the table. When the 3 girls left Shellz said to Damage, "all 3 of them is fine as fuck. Peaches & Cream are 2 cold ass bitches. They gotta be banking that paper."

"Yeah, them some fine twins and Kandy is ice cold. Don't sweat that shit though because the twins are coming to spend the night tonight. I got some other shit to run by you", Damage said.

"Cool, kick it while I listen."

"I was just in the backroom talking to Kandy and she told me that there's a white dude here that owns a few Diamond stores throughout the city and the burbs. The cracker keeps asking her when she is gonna let him take her to the hotel and eat her ass out. He's talking about giving her 2 stacks."

Shellz looked at Damage with a sarcastic look on his face before he asked, "so what's the problem?"

Within A Week

"There really isn't a problem cuz. I don't think you're getting the gist of what I'm saying. This isn't about pimpin or the lousy 2 stacks. I'm thinking of robbing the cracker for some stones. I'm gonna let Kandy hook up with the devil and we're gonna bag his ass. I want to make it really smooth so that we won't have to kill him and at the same time it doesn't look like Kandy set him up."

"How do you expect that to happen?"

"You'll have to play as Kandy's dude. You'll bust into the hotel room and act crazy. You're gonna have to pull the hammer on them and threaten both of them with death. You gotta be sure that the cracker can see the big hole of the hammer in his face. Tell him that you're gonna kill his pink ass for trying to fuck your woman. He'll be shaken and try to make a deal with you. When you burst into the room have your phone on camera status and click off a few shots of his face and Kandy's naked body. Grab his wallet and take out his ID and read off his address and tell him that his wife will see the pictures if he makes it through the night. Then you offer him an ultimatum; which will be $100,000 worth of diamonds or the pictures to his wife", Damage said with sure fact.

"That sounds all good cousin but what if he calls the cops?" Shellz asked with concern.

"I'll follow you into the room with my hat low and head down. When you take his ID you turn and give it to me. I'll leave after that. You & Kandy can handle everything after that. She will pick up if you stumble. She knows how this shit goes."

"Cool. Where would the diamond drop off be and when?"

"Kandy is hooking up with him tonight!! She knows of the diamond drop off spot."

"Damn cuz, we're not gonna practice or rehearse this shit?"

Damage laughed and said, "rehearse? Nigga this ain't no audition for a part in a movie. This shit is just like the shit you did in Florida. Everything is spontaneous. Just go with the flow and it'll be cool. Thrust me, everything will fall into place smoothly."

CHAPTER 8

Damage & Shellz was sitting in Damage's Honda Accord waiting to see Kandy pull into the Hilton Hotel's parking lot. This is the hotel that Kandy brings all of Damage's victims too. To break the silence Shellz said, "how many times have you done this cousin?"

"This is my truest hustle cousin. I hit a lick probably twice a month."

"You must be crazy paid then," Shellz said as he counted some of Damage's money in his head.

"I'm doing alright cuz. I got a few nice things I own."

"Why do you have this whip? You gotta want something better than this!!"

"Believe it or not I own a nice condo. I got a brand new motorcycle that I got with no miles on it. I got a new Corvette and a new Caddy truck."

"Say word cousin."

"Real talk. I'll show off for you in the morning," Damage smiled at him.

Shellz wasn't finished getting in Damage's business so he asked, "what's the deal with Kandy?"

Kandy is my bitch, wifey and best friend. I bought that condo that she lives in too," Damage bragged one more time.

"I would never think that you had all of the things that you have just by looking at you."

Within A Week

"I guess that I'm doing it the way that I want it to be seen. I don't like the limelight. Shining is how you become the target of the Feds, Cops and stick-up kids."

"I know that's right. They say that real killers move like ghost. Have you ever put anybody in the dirt? Even if it was by mistake?"

"Nah cousin, I never killed anybody by mistake. Everybody that I killed, I looked them in the eyes."

"Damn you're cold hearted. How many knockdowns do you have?"

"On some real shit, I can't even tell you how many. I do know that you need 2 hands to count them all on."

"Have you ever been charged with any of them?"

"A dead man can't tell no tales and witnesses don't exist."

"Have you ever shot a nigga up and he survived?"

"Cousin, I shot or stabbed more than I killed."

"Have you ever ran into any of the niggaz that didn't die?"

"Yeah I saw a few of them. I still see a few of them to this day."

"Have any of them ever tried to get back at you?"

"Nah, not really. I shot the bouncer at the strip club back in the day!!"

"For real for real? That's why he practically bowed when we came in?"

"Yeah. His soft ass freeze up whenever I come around."

"You are a wild boy cousin."

"I'm not a wild boy cuz. I just don't play when it comes to life."

"I hear that shit", Shellz said in awe of his cousin.

"Right before you got here I knocked 2 young boyz heads off. A few days before that I had to knock a nigga head off out of state."

"Out of state? Why out of state?"

"Kandy is getting a lot of feature gigs at other strip clubs in other states. The position you're playing tonight with Kandy is my job in other states. Usually they'll take her to their spot because they wanna show off to her. Most of them are usually single and deep in the game. Them the niggaz I don't give another chance to breathe."

"Fuck the bullshit, you crazy cousin."

Damage laughed that remark off and said, "There's Kandy's Range. You ready to get this shit poppin?" Shellz simply nodded that he was ready. "As soon as she gets in there she's gonna crack the side door for us and text me the room number when she is inside the bathroom. On her way out she's gonna unlock the door. Everything else will be like riding a bike."

* * * * *

Kandy got out of her midnight blue Range in a tight fitting purple knee high dress that hugged her curves like a mother hugs her newborn. On her size 6 feet she wore a pair of 6 inch stiletto heels by Prada that made her 5 ft 7 height look Amazonian. She clutched her gator skin handbag close to her body as she elegantly walked over to a pearl white 5 series Benz that was being driven by Conner Stern; the diamond jeweler.

Conner Stern was a 48 year old white Irish American. He was married with 2 children. He was educated and went to college to become a sports agent. He attended college in California and during his college days he discovered his thirst and appetite for black women. He spent most of his time outside of class in various gymnasiums. In every gym he entered there was an abundance of beautiful black women clad in skimpy sports attire that displayed their Phat round asses and juicy titties. Conner wanted a black woman like sinners wants to be saved. He couldn't react to his desires because his parents were paying for his schooling and they were very prejudiced. He was afraid of being cut out of their Will and he knew that if college didn't go according to plan, he would be able to get one of his parents jeweler stores in upstate New York.

One day while sitting on the lawn in front of the library eating lunch in the sunny California weather he saw this beautiful white girl who just so happened to have a body like one of his fantasy black women. Her face was filled with beauty. Her lips were unbelievably full. Her hips flared out to hold a Phat ass. She even had the perfect size tits on her chest. Conner was in awe of seeing a white girl with

Within A Week

such a body. He was used to seeing white girls with huge tits and flat asses. Conner didn't hesitate in going after her. His approach was a mimic of his favorite ball player that had many of the young black women chasing after him. "Excuse me Sunshine!!"

The beautiful girl stopped and faced him. She then asked, "Are you talking to me?"

"Uh…. Yeah, sorry to bother you but I couldn't help but notice how beautiful you are and I couldn't resist the opportunity to introduce myself to you. My name is Conner," he said as he stuck out his hand to shake hers. She took his hand and smiled a warm smile with a chuckle. Conner became offended because of her chuckle and asked, "did I say something amusing?"

"Well, I find it cute that you've dumped your lunch on the lawn to introduce yourself to me Conner. I'm flattered that you chose to meet me over finishing your lunch. Really, I am. My real cause for chuckling is the mixture of mustard and mayo spread over your face."

Conner blushed deeply and tried to remove his hand from hers but she held on tight and pulled him in closer to lick the substance from his mouth. She then said, "my name is Kristen Murphy. It's very nice to meet you Conner. You seem to have a good taste for lunch. Here's my card," she said as she gave him the card. "Call me, we can have lunch someday.

Conner stood statue stiff as he watched Kristen walk away. That was 20 odd years ago. He loved his wife immensely but he was still being haunted with the desire to have a black woman.

* * * * *

Conner got out of his Benz and embraced Kandy with a strong hug. He was very excited that he's finally gonna get a taste of some chocolate pudding. Especially hers. He's been lusting and chasing after her for almost a year now.

"Conner are you sure you want this? I don't want you to do something that you'll regret or can mess things up for you," Kandy said as she played coy.

"I'm 100% sure Angel. I don't want anything more. I only ask that things can be continuous and kept very discreet. I have too much to lose if we're discovered. Here's $3000, get a jacuzzi suit and the rest is yours for your time," Conner said as he handed her an envelope filled with 100 dollar bills.

Kandy took the envelope and entered the hotel to purchase the room. Before going to get Conner she called Damage, "Hey Daddy, everything is all good. We'll be in room 147. It's right next to the swimming pool which happens to be right next to the side door. I'm going to get him now. I'll have him comfortable in a few. Right now it's 2: 41. Y'all can come in at 3:10 exactly. I'll wedge the side door open when we enter the room and I'll unlock the room door after we're settled."

"Alright baby girl. Butter him up and relax him smoothly."

"I always do Daddy," she said.

"Yeah you do baby. Get to your business."

Kandy put her phone away and went to retrieve Conner. As she was approaching, Conner's little white boy dick got hard as the steel found in jails at seeing the black Goddess. She lead him to the side entrance and led him into their suit. Once inside, Conner couldn't keep his paws off of her. He was cupping her phat ass and squeezing her juicy titties as he kissed all over her neck. She wanted him to slow down so she said, "relax sweetheart, let's get comfortable and get in the jacuzzi and sip some of these wine coolers I got for us. Mama's gonna put this sweet pussy on you soon enough."

Conner took a breath and released it. He loosened up his tie and removed his dress shirt. When he was down to his boxers he sat on the edge of the bed and watched as Kandy filled the jacuzzi with bubbled water. When Kandy turned and saw that Conner had relaxed a bit she stripped down to her burgundy thong and bra set. She knew that she had Conner's full attention so she made sure to bend over provocatively for his account. She knew that she was driving him insane. Before she knew what happened she felt strong hands on her ass and her cheeks being spread. She felt her thong being pushed to the side and a warm tongue on her asshole. Her first thought was,

Within A Week

"Damn this cracker can lick ass." She looked at her watch and it read 2:50. She had some time so she allowed Conner to eat her asshole out. She hiked her ass higher so that he could get deeper with his tongue assault. Kandy couldn't believe how talented Conner was with his tongue. She already made up her mind that Conner would be her regular pussy eater. Right before she was about to cum she checked the time and flooded his mouth with a heart hurting orgasm. She stood up and told Conner how good his tongue is and to get in the jacuzzi now that it's ready. She excused herself for a minute and went into the bathroom. Several minutes later she emerged with nothing on but her sexy heels on. Conner's eyes almost exploded out of his head when he saw the Goddess before him. Her body appeared to be smooth and hairless like a baby's. She gently walked to the jacuzzi and got in. Not long after that the room was consumed with Damage and Shellz. Shellz brandished his burner and pointed it at Kandy saying, "you trifling bitch!! What the fuck is going on Kandy?" Shellz was off guard himself because it was the first time that he got to see Kandy naked and he didn't see anyone in the jacuzzi with her. Kandy looked at the dismay on his face and pointed at the water to let him know that Conner was submerged underneath.

Conner had seen the men before they saw him and his first thought was to dip under the water. Shellz walked over to the jacuzzi and tapped Conner on the shoulder. Conner felt the tap and came up from beneath the water and knew that shit might get ugly. Shellz repeated what he asked upon coming into the room just in case Conner didn't hear the first time, "Kandy, what the fuck is going on here? Who is this cracker? Why fuck is you naked in a jacuzzi with this devil?"

Kandy played her part and said, "baby I um... I was just trying to um...."

"Shut the fuck up Bitch!! I'm about to kill both of y'all because of yo trifling ass," as he pointed his burner at them.

"Wait a minute man!! Please just wait a minute. I can make it worthwhile if you just overlook all this. I'm truly sorry for this. I didn't know that she had a boyfriend. She never said anything."

"How can you fix this you dirty cracker?" Shellz addressed Damage when he said, "grab his things and remove his wallet. I wanna know who this devil is that this bitch felt a need to cheat on me with."

Damage got the wallet and read off Conner's information to Shellz and said, "I'm gonna wait outside for you. If you kill them, hurry up."

After Damage left the room Shellz said to Kandy, "get yo funky ass out of that jacuzzi and put some clothes on before I beat yo ass with my burner."

"Okay baby. I'm sorry. Can you let me explain things to you before you kill again?"

"You have less than 3 minutes before this gun goes off and I leave both of y'all here for the cops to find in the morning."

"Baby, this is Conner. He owns a few Diamond stores and I was trying to get a nice deal on a nice chain to surprise you with", she said beginning to cry.

"I don't wanna see them tears. If that's the case why the fuck is yo ass naked in a jacuzzi?"

"He gave me some paper for my time while we discussed it."

"That doesn't explain why yo funky ass is naked!! Why not discuss it at 3 pm instead of 3 am? Why butt naked in a jacuzzi?" "Something ain't right about this picture Bitch. I'm glad that I activated the location on your phone. Did you forget that we were supposed to meet at Denny's after you got off?"

"Oh baby it slipped my mind. I was so intent on making this deal happen that I forgot. I'm sorry Honey."

"Fuck that shit. Yo ass gon be sorry. You too white boy", Shellz said as he cocked his burner.

Hearing the bullet slide into the chamber caused Conner to find his voice. He said, "NO NO Wait!! Let me help change your mind. How about if I just give you the diamonds that your girl here is talking about? No charge at all if you just forget that any of this happened."

Shellz looked Conner in the eyes and asked, "how much are these diamonds worth?"

"20 grand easily."

Within A Week

"You're trying to tell me that your life is only worth 20 grand?"

"I can do a bit more if I need to."

"Let me remind you of something white boy. My partner has your ID with him. We know where you live. Kandy, go over there and let me take a few pictures of you with him so I can send his wife." After Shellz clicked off a few pictures he said, "I'll show your wife these pics and she'll demand more than what I'm demanding. I want you to give Kandy 200 grand worth of diamonds tomorrow night. If she come home without them you'll hear about her murder on the news and you'll know that I'll be coming for you next."

"Okay.... I can manage that. She'll get the diamonds tomorrow."

Shellz turned to Kandy and said, "get yo shit you trifling bitch. You got every bit of 90 seconds to have yo shit or I'll change my mind and kill y'all."

* * * * *

Walking into her condo with Shellz right behind her she yelled, "Daddy!! We're here Daddy."

Damage yelled down from the master bedroom, "I'm up here gorgeous."

Kandy turned to Shellz and said, "you did a great job. The kitchen is that way and the guest room is that way. There's a bar in the living room. Make yourself at home", she said as she headed to her King.

Shellz was on his way to the bar when he heard water splashing from a room off the hallway. He opened the door and saw that the twins Peaches & Cream was in a jacuzzi with a bottle of Remy on the stand next to it. Shellz smiled and flew out of his gear. Peaches looked at Shellz meat and said to her twin, "no more wondering if he has enough for the both of us."

"It surely looks like he has enough. The only question that remains is can he keep it up long?" Cream said to her twin.

Shellz smiled and said, "y'all not gon talk around me in front of me. Hell yeah I have enough dick for both of y'all and I can make it last until y'all fine ass is delirious off this dick."

Cream laughed and said, "talk that shit Shellz."

"I'm not talking shit bitch. Pour some of that Remy on this dick and get to sucking it off!!"

"Hell yeah Daddy, talk that talk", Peaches said as she grabbed the Remy and poured some on his dick and began sucking it.

* * * * *

"So how did Shellz do baby?" Damage asked Kandy as he rubbed her body.

"He did really well. Conner is gonna bring me 200 grand of diamonds tomorrow."

"Say word!! How did y'all pull that off?"

"The fact that you left with his ID and he had a pistol in his face."

"That's what's up. Do you think he'll follow through?"

"Yeah…. Conner will bring the stones tomorrow. He was too scared not to."

"Cool…. You know that I love you right?"

"I know you do Daddy. I never doubt that. Even if you don't tell me often."

"So what's been going on at the club lately?"

"Same ole shit really. There's been a few new old heads though that's been trying to get at me. I'll have a line on a few of them sooner than later."

"Cool. Here, put this paper up and let's go fuck with Shellz before we crash."

"Alright Daddy. Oh yeah, Peaches & Cream haven't called me yet but they should be here shortly."

"They're here already. When I pulled up a cab pulled up at the same time. They're probably in the gameroom playing pool with Shellz as we speak."

"So let's leave them alone and let me give you what I got for you?" Kandy said as she pushed him back and pulled out his dick.

CHAPTER 9

Dr. Corzine showed up to do his rounds promptly at 6 am. He made his way to Chester Chambers room. His chart showed that Chester was in grave condition and death was around the corner. When a doctor I've never seen before showed up in my room I thought this was the doctor here to bring me my signing out papers. He looked at me like he was seeing a ghost. He looked at his chart and said, "Mr. Chambers, how are you feeling this morning? You look good considering."

"I guess I'm feeling as good as I'm looking. Are you here to give me my walking papers?"

"That's definitely the attitude to have. Are you in any discomfort or pain?"

"Just minor pain. Nothing that my own bed can't soothe."

The doctor looked perplexed, "Mr. Chambers you do know how vital your situation is right?"

"Vital? I don't think that vital is the correct word but I'm cool regardless."

"I don't think that you fully understand your condition."

"Sure I do. I have a few busted ribs and a sore chest", I said.

"That's true. You also have been diagnosed with grave cancer. I'm assuming that you don't know that you have no more than a week to live?"

That shit right there really blew my mind!! All I was able to do was sit back with my mouth open looking dumbfounded. I was thinking to myself how can I have cancer? Wouldn't I feel terrible walking around with that deadly disease? Wouldn't there be some type of symptoms that'll reveal something was wrong with me? This shit can't be true….. I'm a young healthy nigga. The doctor gotta have mixed up some shit up by mistake. So I opened my eyes and said, "Doc, are you certain that your files are correct?"

"I'm quite certain. Were you in a form of auto accident?"

"Yeah. I was."

"Is your name Chester Chambers?"

"Yeah. I'm Chester Chambers."

"Well, I'm sorry to inform you that you are whom I'm talking about. You are the only Chester Chambers here who've been admitted with a form of auto accident. I'm sorry young man but you will be needing more tests. Releasing you will be out of the question today."

I sat back and let my mind digest this horrific information. Something inside me is telling me that the good ole doctor is giving me false information. As the doctor exited the room I summoned the nurse that was on duty. Within seconds an overweight white nurse entered my room. She looked at me and said, "good morning Mr. Chambers. What can I do for you this morning?"

"Good morning, Miss nurse. I was just wondering if my checkout time is on the computer?"

"I'll check in just a minute. Can I get you something to drink while I'm out?"

"No thank you. That requested information will do."

Five minutes later the nurse wobbled back into the room with the information I asked for. "Unfortunately Mr. Chambers there is no release time for you on the computer. From my research your illness is very serious. You are scheduled to be moved to another part of the Hospital that can better cater to your condition."

Just searching for more information I asked, "condition? What condition are you referring to?"

"You've been diagnosed with grave cancer sir."

"That's bullshit lady!! Look at me!! I'm fucking healthy as a newborn. I breathe easy. I have my hair and I'm not in any real pain

Within A Week

except for my damaged ribs, which came from the accident. You people are making a mistake. Y'all got me mixed up with someone else", I scream at the fat bitch with the misinformation.

"I'm sorry that you're going through this sir. Really I am. I'm only delivering the information that's in our computer."

I've heard enough of this bullshit so I said, "Thank you. Can you please excuse me? I'd like some time to myself to think."

"Sure Mr. Chambers. Again I'm sorry." The nurse said as she found the door knob.

As soon as she left I pulled out my celly and hit Sleaze on the hip. He answered right away, "What up Big Homie? It ain't even 7 yet. What's good?"

"Ain't shit good Lil Homie."

"Why? What's up?"

"The hospital is making a big mistake. They must've gotten my charts mixed up with someone elses or something. These muthafuckaz are trying to move me to the Cancer patient floor my nigga."

"The cancer floor? What did they go do some shit like that for? They must've found out that you a ILL nigga", Sleaze said jokingly.

"Now is not the time for jokes my dude."

"You being serious Chips?"

"Hell yeah..... They said that I have cancer bruh."

"They said WHAT? It was all good yesterday."

"Tell me about it. Fuck what these people talking about, I need you to get up here like yesterday. They're planning on moving me a little later. I'm not going for any of that shit."

"I'm leaving the house right now. I'll be there within 10 min. Be ready to breeeze."

"Alright my nigga. I'll see you in a bit", I told him as we ended the call.

I hung up the phone and started gathering the few items that I felt I needed. I slipped on my Nike sweats, my ones and a crispy white tee. I walked to the nurses station and told the nurse there that I wanted to stretch my legs and I'm taking a few laps around the floor. Her phone rang at the same time so she nodded to me that it was cool so I began my walk to escape. (Am I the only one that finds it crazy that I gotta escape from the hospital?) I walked around the nurse's station 3 times before my phone vibrated in my sweats. I rounded a corner and entered an elevator and headed downstairs to the back exit. When the elevator got to the ground floor I calmly went out the doors and poured into Sleaze's whip.

"Chips, what the fuck is going on my nigga?"

"I don't know what the fuck is going on but if it's true that I'm dying within a week I'm turning shit up in the streets."

Sleaze started smiling before he said, "yeah my nigga!! You already know what it is with me. I'm riding shotgun for this shit!!"

"I already know that yo wild ass is down to go for the whole 4 quarters. Run me to the building so I can shower and get my mind straight." Sleaze pulled into my driveway 20 minutes later. Before I hopped out of the whip I sent Sleaze to get the work that he got from Damage and bring it here. He said nothing but shook his head and bounced.

Once inside my building I checked my safes and gun cabinets. Once I found everything to be the way it should I reset the alarm and jumped in the shower. The steaming hot water did exactly what I needed it to do for my mental. I used the water to hide my tears and penetrate my thoughts so I can create a trickle effect on the city. I came up with the perfect plan that's gonna leave my peoples on full deck when I do die. I decided to get at every bitch-ass nigga that ever crossed me, every bitch that disrespected me and I'm gonna walk, rob and take hella dope from every nigga that's moving weight in the city. Niggaz gonna respect my G or wear red tee's. It's simple as that.

After I got dressed, Sleaze pulled into the driveway. I opened to let him in before he even got out of the car. Once inside he dumped the duffle bag on the floor and said, "That's the work and some bread from Ray-Ray, Otis and Big John. I gave each of them a quarter brick of the last shit. They should be ready for you later tonight or tomorrow morning the latest."

Within A Week

"Alright. That's what's up. How are you for bread?"

"I'm good for bread. I wanna know what we're gonna get into."

"C'mon", I said to my lil homie and lead him in the basement. He's never been down there before. Nobody has ever been down there. That's where I keep the safes and guns. I have 3 safes there and 2 big gun cabinets full of all types of shit. In this dope game you gotta cop every weapon that crosses your path. Even if you're a laid back, cool nigga like me. Don't get things twisted though; I'm easy going but I've put a coupla dicks in the dirt!! Them niggaz deserved it. Anyway, the reason for all my artillery was mainly for protection. Now it's for destruction.

I had all my weapons spread out on a table already. When Sleaze stepped off the bottom step he gasped and smiled the lottery winning smile before saying, "Hell Yeah!! Damn big homie, what the fuck is all this?"

"This is what I've been collecting over the years."

"Damn dawg, I didn't know you had this shit."

"You know I've been seeing that bread in the game. My first rule is have your arsenal on point for the snakes that are slithering in the uncut grass."

"Yeah, you right", Sleaze said as his eyes roamed over the table. "Wait.... What the fuck is that right there Chips?" He pointed to my M-1 with the grenade launcher attached to it.

I smiled at him and said, "Remember the end of Scarface when Sosa sent his goons to get at Tony Montana? When Scarface said, "say hello to my little friend", and sent a rocket flying? Well, my nigga, this is the very same gun!!"

"This joint look crazy as fuck. How did you come up with this joint bruh? I want one of these bruh."

"With what the doctors are saying, that's gonna be yours. You can get familiar with it because I'm about to turn all the way up and leave you with everything. Riches and death are around the corner for me, what comes first remains to be seen."

"Chips you don't have to tell me the plan, all you gotta do is count me in. If I get rich; cool. If I die trying; cooler. Whatever it is, I'm riding with you until the wheels fall off."

"That's what's up. Be on point really hard because I'm about to be erratic and reckless!!"

CHAPTER 10

I looked at my phone to see what time it was. It was damn near 10 and I haven't eaten yet. It felt like my stomach was touching my back. We jumped in my low-key and headed to eat. We were going down Box toward Fillmore on our way to Matties. We parked and snatched our pistols from the stash spot and placed them in our waistband. We went inside and were seated immediately. A sexy hoodrat came to take our order. Both of us had a double stack of pancakes, scrambled eggs, grits, corned beef hash, OJ and a large milk.

After we finished busting down our food we sat back and allowed our food to digest a bit before bouncing. Sad to say that 3 young boyz came in and were being unruly. The waitress told them it will be a 5 min wait to be seated due to table cleaning. The 3 boyz wasn't trying to hear that and let it be known. One of them looked at our table. The waitress had cleaned our table up after we ate and enjoyed a hefty tip afterwards and knew of us letting our food digest a bit. The nigga that looked at our table said, "them 2 niggaz right there are done. They can get the fuck up and let some real niggaz sit down." The waitress gasped at the rudeness of the comment and politely told him that we weren't done yet. I guess her statement triggered something within the mind of one of dudes homie because he yelled across the room and said, "A yo, y'all 2 bird niggz done over there? A few Real niggaz is trying to eat!!"

Sleaze is a wild boy by nature. He's always ready for that daytime action anywhere and anytime. He was definitely down to open up and leave them niggaz stiff at the front door. I saw that Sleaze was slowly reaching for his waist so I told him that it was cool because these 3 fools didn't know that they're about to breathe their last breaths.

* * * * *

When we got into the car I said to Sleaze, "pull off and circle the block. Wrap around and park on the corner of Box so we can see them clowns when they come out."

"Word… I got you."

Sleaze pulled off and turned on Glenwood and took it down to Kehr then turned right and another right on Box. He eased close to the corner of Box and Fillmore to watch Matties. It was close to an hour before them 3 dead men came out. They jumped into a nice 300M. It looked brand new. That explained to me the cockiness. Getting paper can change some niggaz. I bet they think they run the city now because they were seeing some bread. Well, I'm about to put an end to their cockiness!!

The driver was a tall, naturally cocky dude who just came home from prison. He's been home for about 5 months and got right into that paper. A lot of dudes who do prison time seem to get big and think that their size will intimidate others.

The other 2 niggaz with him was his 'Do Boyz' or Flunkies if you call it that. When the head nigga say move, they move without hesitation. The head nigga can say 'Jump' and them niggaz turn into grasshoppers. They thought their Boss was invincible; that's why they were acting fools in Matties.

Watching the 3 niggaz walking to the 300M and their demeanors told me a lot about them. They were fronting!! They didn't really want problems but it was too late for that shit now. As fate has it, these 3 pussies are about to be fucked.

"Get a few cars behind them Sleaze. When I give you the word I want you to pull right beside them."

Within A Week

"Bruh... How about you drive and let me do the clapping? You know I haven't put in work in a minute. I need it bad homie."

"Nah lil nigga, I got this one. You can get the next bird that flaps his wings recklessly."

"Bet."

We followed the 300M down to Ferry. These fools were oblivious to being followed. They turned left and headed towards Bucktown. They passed Wholers and stopped at the light at Jefferson. They then turn right headed towards Delavan. At the next street they turn right and pullover in front of a nice looking two story house. "Give me your 40 and pull mup right next to them. I want you to stop the car right next to them", I told Sleaze.

"Say no more", Sleaze said as he gave me his 40.

We pulled up beside the dead men. Before Sleaze had the car at a full stop I was already hanging out the window. The driver was the first to notice me. The look on his face was priceless. He looked at my face and then at the pair of hammers in my hands. I couldn't hear him but I read his lips and it looked like he said, "OH SHIT!!". That's when he saw the first flash of many as the 40 & 44 opened up. The first shot hit him in the center of his face. The second one tore his head from his neck. I re-aimed at the flunky in the front with him and he tried to curl into a small ball but got hit like 7 times for his efforts. The nigga in the back had wisely jumped out of the car. He had a pistol in his hand but his thoughts weren't about war; it was about running. I hit him in the calf to stop his flight. He fell to the ground and his burner flew out of his hands. I opened the door and ran up on him and dumped 3 well placed shots to the back of his head. Knowing that my death will be later this week I didn't breeze outta there but took my time and relieved all of them for their jewels and cash. I got such a rush from this shit that I knew the town was in for some shit.

CHAPTER 11

As we circled back to the hood I sat in the car very quietly and in deep thought. Sleaze must've thought that I was worried or thinking about the 3 clowns I left stiff because he said, "Chips, are you alright my nigga?"

"Yeah I'm cool."

"Don't feel bad about them 3 dead niggaz. They deserve what they got."

"I'm not trippin over them fools."

"Why are you so quiet then? What's on your mind?"

"I was just thinking how life really holds no substance. At any given time shit can change and it usually does. Three days ago I never would've knocked them niggaz heads off over that bullshit in Matties. Today and until my last breath any and everybody who violates will get their heads knocked off. Shit, muthafuckaz won't even have to violate to meet Jesus."

"You did a total change with your character. What brought it about?"

"Them fucking crooked doctors told me that I have terminal Cancer and I'm gonna die within a week."

"Damn bruh, I didn't know it was this serious. I'm sorry to hear this shit. Bullshit always happen to good niggaz", Sleaze said with passion.

"Thanks for the condolences but I need you to fully understand what's going on in my head. As I was saying bruh, life changes everyday. Just think about it, mine will be over by this time next week. The thing that's bothering me the most is that I'm bringing you into something that you probably aren't down for. I need and want you to make the conscious decision on your own to roll with me or not. It wouldn't be fair to me to dictate what path your life takes."

"Listen big homie, it's whatever with me. You already know that you're all I have. You took off the street and showed me nothing but love. You fed me, clothed me and taught me how to eat and live in this cold cold world. My own biological father didn't even hold my bottle to feed me. My mother sold the food from our freezer to support her addiction. Man, I owe you everything and I'd give you anything. So whatever changes my life may take while fucking with you big homie, let the chips fall where they may. I got your back till the end!!"

Hearing Sleaze tell me that leads me into a reserved state of mind. I knew that whatever happened he would hold me down. At the same time I gotta do everything I can to make sure he lives through all the bullshit that I'm about to indulge in so he can enjoy life with everything that is accumulated from all the violence that's coming. I gotta be articulate and careful. I can't allow myself to become reckless like I was just a short time ago when I killed them 3 fools.

* * * * *

Damage got up early as he's accustomed too and ventured down to his guest room in the condo only to find Shellz asleep in between the twins. Damage had a fat dutch in his lips as he walked over to the stereo system and turned on WBLK. The sudden noise awoke the trio with a start. Shellz mumbled, "what the fuck?!" The twins chimed in with, "Damage can you please? We're so fucking tired! Your cousin here isn't human." Damage laughed and handed Shellz the lit dutch and yanked the covers off of the bed. Shellz tried to cover himself while the twins just remained motionless. He told the twins to get up and get in the bed with Kandy. The girls rolled out of bed and didn't bother to grab clothes but headed to the door naked. Peaches turned before exiting and said to Shellz, "we had a great time Daddy. Hopefully we'll be able to enjoy more of you sooner than later." Shellz smiled and said, "no doubt sweetheart, we'll get up later." Damage tossed the cover back to Shellz and demanded the dutch back. Several minutes later Damage and Shellz were at the kitchen table eating waffles. Damaged asked, "how was your night cuz?"

"Everything was above par. Shit was really smooth."

"Kandy told me how you handled that cracker."

"Yeah, that shit was really easy. Easier than I thought."

"Easier how? Tell me something about it."

"For starters, the whole scheme went flawless and effortless. Yo girl was a pro with the shit. I fell right into my role."

"So you're a modern day actor huh man?"

"I won't go that far with it but I will say this though, I managed to make that cracker kick in 200 g's worth of diamonds instead of the 100 like planned."

"Kandy said that. Y'all did really well. I'm gonna chop you out with some rocks when we get our hands on them."

"That's what's up."

"You down with rollin to Cleveland with us tonight? Kandy and the twins have a show to do out there tonight and tomorrow night."

"I'm with you in everything, cousin. You don't even have to ask; just drive and I'm in. What time are we leaving?"

"I gotta hit the streets first to see what's shaking and moving. After that we can hit the road."

"How long is the ride?"

"Maybe 4 or 5 hours."

"Why are we gonna be leaving so early then?"

"The girls gotta shop and I'm planning on hitting up SixFlags for some fun first."

"Okay, that's what's up. What do you have on the streets besides that Chips work?"

"Nothing really. I'm just gonna load up on some more smoke."

Within A Week

"Speaking of smoke, what the fuck was that we was just puffing on? That shit right there was some real fire."

"That was some shit called pineapple express. Them niggaz from Box n Moe got that shit."

"Box n Moe? What's that?" Shellz asked.

"That's a block in the hood. That block only deals in the good green. That's where the nigga Chips is from."

"Oh…. I'm ready to roll when you are."

"Cool. Come on", Damage said as he led Shellz out of the condo and to an elevator. Inside the elevator Damage pushed the button to the basement and led Shellz to a royal blue Corvette. Shellz admired the sportscar before saying, "this muthafucka is pretty as fuck cousin. You got a little style hidden within all that gangsta shit huh cuz?"

"I told you bruh, I do me. I just don't broadcast my shit in the streets."

"Word. I hear that."

Damage pointed in a corner and said, "my bike is over there and my Caddy truck is in the garage at my building. That's where we're going now. I'm taking the Vette, get in."

They hopped in and headed over to Box n Moe to see Gator and Dawg. They're the ones with that Pineapple Express shit. Several years ago Gator had formed a crew within the Box n Moe outfit called the Caddy Boyz!! It consisted of Gator, Zack(rip) and Dawg. They are my niggaz til the end. We just don't hang much. They had a white boy hitting them with that piff until shit turned ugly. Somehow them boyz still got that smoke.

Damage pulled up to the house in the middle of the block and hopped out of the car. As usual, my block was flooded with young hustlers and killers alike. My hood knew who Damage was and what he was about. When he jumped out of the Vette all the shooters focused their attention on him, his movements and his pretty whip. Damage called Gator's cell to let him know that he was outside the building. Gator and Dawg came on the porch to meet Damage. Gator said, "Damage, what's good my nigga?"

"Everything. Always. Dawg, what's up my G?"

"Coolin as usual sun. I see that today must be a good day for you to bring out that pretty Vette."

"Yeah, that joint is looking real sexy. Who's in the car?" Gator asked.

"That's family. My cousin from Florida," replied Damage.

"Alright… What can I do for you today bruh?" Gator asked.

"I'm trying to get a QP of that Pineapple shit."

"I got it. You have the numbers on it though right?"

"You want 2 stacks right?" Damage asked, knowing he was wrong.

Dawg spoke up first, "you're off by a stack."

"Damn my niggaz, 3 stacks for a QP?"

"Yeah my nigga, you know that we're the only niggaz on the east coast with this shit."

Damage only had 3 stacks on him and didn't want to give it all up so he said, "All I have is 3 stacks on me. Let me walk away with it for 28?"

Without hesitation Gator invited him into the house. Damage scanned the area real subtle like and noticed over 6 guns scattered throughout the house. Ever since our friend Zack was murdered Gator and Dawg bought every gun that crossed their paths. Damage said, "Damn Dawg, it looks like they are ready for war!!"

"We stay ready for war," Dawg said as he revealed his bulletproof vest and 50 cal.

"I can dig it. The streets really don't love anybody. Especially when the streets are full of broke niggaz looking to die over shit that they don't even believe in."

"I couldn't say it better," Gator replied.

As damage and Dawg continued tossing it up Gator was putting that Pineapple on the scale. After measuring out the amount to equal Damage's money he put it in a plastic baggy and handed it to Damage. Damage pulled out his cash and gave Gator the 2800. As Damage was putting the smoke in his pocket he looked at the monitors on the screen and picked out the shooters. He looked at

Gator and said, "I see all the extra shooters out there. Y'all boyz got some beef?"

"Nah... Them lil niggaz are just holding their block down," Dawg replied.

"I hear that. Y'all breeding some soldiers huh man?"

"This is just the way our hood is," Gator said as he walked Damage out of the house.

Back in his whip, Damage said to Shellz, "these boyz got shit on lock over here. The 2 niggaz I was talking to is Gator and Dawg. Them the bud boyz. Chips is their boy from the ground up. This is a bud block. Chips have a coke spot on every block in this hood except this one. All the lil niggaz you see out here are fully strapped and ready to die for their hood. They are cool. They all move as 1 though. You beef with one, you got beef with them all. Next time we come through here I'll introduce you to the bud boyz so you can come on your own if you need to. Here, smell this funky shit here," Damage gave Shellz the Pineapple.

Shellz took the bag and simply smiled at the color alone. He then said, "I've never seen any yellow bud before. What the fuck is this shit cousin?" Shellz asked Damage. "What is it called and can we get more?"

"They call it Pineapple express. They're the only niggaz on the east coast with that shit. When we come back from Cleveland we'll cop some more; until then my nigga roll a fat one for us."

CHAPTER 12

As Sleaze and I rounded the corner of Box n Moe I saw Damage coming my way. In his passenger seat sat some dude I never saw before. They were talking and didn't notice us. As we passed each other Sleaze said, "Wasn't that Damage right there?"

"Yeah. Is that his cousin with him?"

"Yeah. that's dude."

"Oh yeah? I wonder why he didn't call me with him being on my block."

"He probably thinks you're at home resting."

"Yeah… Probably."

Sleaze never saw Damage's Corvette so he asked, "that's his whip?"

"Yeah… That joint tough huh man?"

"Hell yeah… That bitch is hard as fuck."

"He got a few toys. Wait until you see his Escalade."

"He's getting paper like that?" Sleaze asked.

"Yeah… Fuck him though. Pull up to Gator and Dawg so I can grab some of that funny looking shit they got."

As I got outta the car and before I can get to Gator and Dawg's spot I was approached by a young nigga named Black. Black said, "Hey Chips, what's poppin OG?"

"Man, who the hell are you calling OG? Do yo young ass even know what OG stands for?" I asked the young nigga before me.

"Yeah… I know what an OG is."

Within A Week

"What is a OG lil nigga?"

"A OG is a older nigga that bangs with the best of them."

I just laughed at the lil nigga. He thought he was smart. The lil nigga is a good kid and he has all the potential to be a boss nigga one day. Right now he's playing his position as a shooter for Gator & Dawg. He wanna roll with me so bad though. Every time I see him he keeps asking if he can roll with me. He asked, "when is you & Sleaze gonna let me ride and get some bread with y'all? You can just use me to Blam on niggaz. I'm nice with a knife but official with my pistol!!"

"Black, you're not ready for this life I'm living. In another few years you'll be ready."

"Bruh, I'm ready now!! Come get me and I'll prove to you how real shit is over here with me. I can show you better than I can tell you."

"I hear you lil nigga. Until then, hold the block down." Dawg & Gator appeared on the porch. Dawg said to Sleaze, "Aye Sun, what up with you fool? What ya rich niggaz doing?"

"We ain't no rich niggaz fool. What's up with y'all? Y'all the rich niggaz."

"We just chillin, trying to get it like the Mexicans. Same shit different day."

"No doubt. What's up with a game of Madden? We can play for a young $50." Sleaze said to Dawg.

"Say no more Sun." Dawg said and turned to me saying, "Chips, what up Sun? How are you feeling? I heard about the accident. Are you good?"

"I'm good bruh. How are you?"

"Cool as usual."

"That's what's up."

Sleaze & Dawg dipped into the house to play the game and left me and Gator on the porch. Gator looked me over and said, "what's really hood my nigga? You don't look too good my nigga. You still in pain?"

"Man I'm in pain but it's not physical." I said to them.

"Word? Kick it while I listen."

"What I'm about to tell you I need you to keep it on the hush from everyone but Dawg."

"Say no more. What's up?"

"I've learned some bullshit after that accident. The doctors took blood and did a few tests. This morning a doctor came to my room and told me that I have terminally ill cancer cells in my body. They said that I'll be dead within a week."

"Get the fuck outta here nigga. Stop playing my G."

"I wish I was playing. I wish they were playing. On everything I love my nigga, I was told that this morning."

"Damn Chips, I'm really sorry to hear this shit bruh. What's the next move? What can I do for you my nigga? Just name it!!"

"I don't really need too much of anything really. I'm gonna turn it up in the streets. I'll just need a shooter or 2. Is there anything you need done? I'm turning in all debts and disses."

"I'm good my dude. You need shooters for?"

"I've told you my nigga. The streets are mine. I'm taking everything and leaving whoever rolls with me on full."

"You can take any shooter you want. You want Dawg?"

"Nah, Dawg is your right hand. Besides, when the smoke clear y'all probably gotta put more heads to bed."

"What makes you say that my nigga?"

"Niggaz know where I'm from and they know who I fucks with. Some nigga might feel a certain way once I die and they can't get to me."

"I hear that. Niggaz don't really wanna go there with us though. We kill parents and kids to draw a nigga outta hiding."

"Just so you know, I owe that nigga Damage for 10 bricks."

"Damage??? How'd that happen? He don't fuck with work!!"

"He got a cousin that came from Florida with some fire work."

"Oh.. Okay. Damage just came through here for some smoke. That must've been the cousin in the car with him. So you owe for 10 bricks, you got that bread right?" Gator asked.

"I didn't even touch the work yet but I do have the bread to pay him if I want to. I'm on some fuck him and his cousin shit. Fuck them niggaz!!"

"Chips, you do know that he'll come gunning for you right my dude?"

"That's cool with me G. I'm dying within a week remember? Besides, if he doesn't come correct it's gonna be his dick that's put in the dirt."

"No doubt."

"On some real shit my G; you already know how I painted the town red back in the day. My guns still go off. I just had them on pause while I paper chase."

Gator tried to ease some tension as he said, "nigga you've been getting paper for so long that you probably forgot how to even load the hammer!!"

I smiled and said, "Busting my hammer is unforgettable. Between us, I knocked off the 3 clowns this morning."

"Them niggaz off of Jefferson?"

"Yeah yeah."

"Say word!!"

"Real talk!! I ran into them clowns at Matties and they were acting stronger than coffee in there."

"What happened bruh?"

"They tried to clown me and Sleaze. They thought we were sweet."

"They must've thought that."

"Yeah well. Gator be careful out there. Put yo niggaz on full alert. Stay humble my nigga. You a good dude and the streets are full of angry broke niggaz. If you gotta put a nigga to bed, don't hesitate or wait. Get right to it."

"Thanks bruh, but I'm good. I'm good with mine. Dawg is good with his and Zack is watching over us. We're good and ready for war."

"That's what's up. RIP Zack!! Just know that my moves aren't intended to bring harm your way or to our block. Forgive me if shit gets hectic."

"Don't sweat none that shit bruh. You my nigga until our last breath. If you want, me and Dawg can ride with you my nigga. Life means nothing my nigga."

"That's not necessary. Just keep living and enjoying life bruh. What you can do is smoke some of that good shit and sell me a few O's."

"C'mon, let's get fucked up with our gunners. I got a few O's for you on GP."

"Thanks, but I rather pay you for a few O's because I can't take this money to hell with me!"

CHAPTER 13

Before leaving from the block Gator gave me 2 O's of that bomb smoke and his lil soldier Black. That lil nigga was excited to roll with me for some reason. While Sleaze drove; going nowhere fast, I quizzed Lil Black on a few things. The first question I asked was, "why do you wanna hang out with me so bad?"

"Because you like to move around and go places outside the hood."

"We're about our business lil nigga. We don't do it for fun. We are on a massive paper chase. We don't have fun for real. Our moving around is really throwing rocks at the prisons."

"I have an idea of what you do and I wanna learn how to do what you do. I need to do something more than sitting on the block waiting for some fools to come through and violate."

"What if some fools did come through on some violating shit?"

"I highly doubt that niggaz is stupid but if some fools did come through it'll be their ass. I'm 16 and I don't give a fuck about shit!! My gun goes off like a whistle in the NBA. I'd down any & every nigga that violates or disrespect any & all that I hold dear to my heart. I'm a Box n Moe nigga from birth. I grew here while others flew here. I rep Box n Moe to the fullest and I pray that the world doesn't make me end it because the world will end!!"

"I hear that lil nigga. Box is our world."

"You better believe that shit OG."

"On a different note Black, I trust Sleaze with my life and I'd give my life for Sleaze. Are you ready to kill and die for me Black? That's what's going on with me right now lil homie. Things ain't what you know it to be. The end result will be a big blessing though because the means of getting this bread is a bit different from the norm."

"Whatever it is you can count me in. It doesn't matter what is going on, I'm with you regardless."

"Alright lil nigga, you sure that you ready for this life? Your life is gonna change drastically from this point on. Your gun will be active constantly. Are you ready for a constant life and death situation?"

"Bruh, I'm ready to ride for my OG."

I liked this little nigga Black. I didn't tell him about my personal situation with the Cancer. He didn't need to know that. All he wanted to do was roll and that's what we were going to do. He wanna bust his gun and I'm gonna give him the opportunity sooner than later.

Sleaze was heading to Money Mike's spot in the Fruitbelt. The Fruitbelt is a neighborhood that has every street named after a fruit. Niggaz over there really get it in. Some live wires came out of there. Most of them are mad crazy. I mean it literally too… They're crazy and mad that Mike is from there but get all his bread from moving my work. Back in the days the police wouldn't even venture through the fruitbelt. On 2 different occasions 4 officers were gunned down in the fruitbelt. Cop cars would stop at a stop sign and some wild nigga would run up on the cops and unload a fully loaded clip from a AK-47 and chop the coppers in half!!

Sleaze and I haven't been through here in almost a month. The last time we came through I kinda got pressed by one of those crazy ass niggaz as I went to pick up my bread from Money Mike. It was done by some young boyz looking for a come up. I was too hard on my grind and let them best me and left the bread with Money Mike. That shit didn't sit well with Sleaze though. I had to keep him focused on the bigger picture and allow them clowns to keep that small change. He wanted to go to war with them but I was more intuned with stacking more bread. Today however, I didn't have to tell Sleaze to come this way. He knew that I was ready for all the beef and he's been holding that incident in for a while now. Mike owed me 8 stacks and Sleaze was determined to get it. So was I. I was actually happy and thrilled that we were heading there. It was time that Money Mike paid his debt to me and God. Black will get his chance to put his gun to work for me.

As Sleaze pulled up behind Money Mikes Volvo I turned to Black and told him, "Take the safety off your hammer and pay close attention. You might get to prove yourself right away. It's a green light on anybody that gets out of line." We got out of the car and headed to the back where Money Mike usually held it down. I knocked on the door like I was the police. Mike came to the door and asked, "Who dat?"

"It's Chips nigga, open up."

Mike opened the door and smiled a retarded smile before saying, "Hey Chips, what's good bruh? How are you doing?"

"I'm good Mike. Can I come in?" I ask.

"Yeah... C'mon in," he says as he steps to the side. Sleaze goes in first then me and Black follow. After locking the door behind us, Mike leads us to the living room where Mike was chillin before we interrupted him. He takes a seat on his lounge chair and offers us a seat.

We declined a seat and I said, "We don't plan on being long bruh. I came for those 8 bands you owe me."

He looked at me with puzzlement in his eyes. He looked like a deer caught in headlights. Before he started to tell me a lie or some other bullshit I said, "I'm not here for any games Mike. I have no time for lies. I don't give a fuck about none of them young boyz that's out on the corner either. You have just 2 options right now; get my bread to me or meet God."

Hearing me give him his options and none was appealing to him and with Black pulling out the biggest pistol that I ever saw a lil nigga hold, Mike looked at the big pistol and then at me and said, "I got some bread in the trunk of my car. Let me run to it and grab the bread I owe you?! I'll even toss you out a lil something for your wait."

"Just give Sleaze your keys and he'll go get what's in there and bring it back. If everything is everything then everything will be cool, the way I wanna keep it. If something not you'll see a different Chips than you know. Give Sleaze the keys."

Mike hesitated for just a second but readjusted his position and pulled his keys from his pocket and tossed them to Sleaze. Sleaze was gone for about 2 minutes before he came back smiling. He dropped the bag on the floor and said, "I saw them lil niggaz on the corner gathering together. We gotta be on full point when we leave here."

Black focused hard on Mike as I squatted down to rifle through the bag. Inside the bag was 2 mac-10's and a long nosed .357. He also had at least 150 bands in the bag too. I was feeling kinda proud of Money Mike for the way he grinded. I knew he was getting bread but I was happy to see that he was going hard. I was still a player until the day I died so I took my 8 stacks and asked, "how much are you giving me for the wait?"

He looked at me and said, "just take 15 more stacks and we cool?!"

"That's what's up Mike. I knew you were a good dude. That's why I fucked with you." I removed the 15 bands and the guns then tossed the bag to Mike. He looked into the bag and showed a lot of joy seeing that he had his bread in his clutches. As Mike admired his bread I winked at Sleaze and said, "Mike, these dudes need to get paid also. I refuse to pay them out of my bread because of your fuck up."

"It's cool," Mike said as he tossed Sleaze and Black 5 stacks each.

Of course Sleaze was being Sleaze and said, "This not enough player."

"What do you mean player? It's a free 5 bands," Mike tried to reason.

"Did I stutter nigga? This ain't enough!!"

Mike looked to me for help and said, "Chips, what's up with ya man? I thought you said everything was gonna be cool?"

"Everything is cool between us!! That's just us."

"C'mon Chips, don't do me like that bruh."

"It's not me bruh. I'm not going out like nothing. We're cool. I'm not talking to you; Sleaze is playboy."

Black spoke for the first time and said, "enough of all this talking shit." Then he opened Mike's chest cavity. The roar of Black's burner was deafening. For several seconds I couldn't hear shit. I told Sleaze to put the macs in the bag with the bread and I put the tre pound in my waistband. We left and averted going past the corner where we knew we'd have to go to war. Black held the bag in the backseat and asked, "how do you want me to split this bread up OG?"

"Just split it in half. I got my cut already. Take out 20 stacks so I can give to Gator & Dawg. The rest is for you niggaz."

"You serious Chips? I never had this kind of bread before."

"Well, enjoy it later. You did good back there. We're gonna come across a lot more paper on this ride. Just stay true to the game and you'll be running shit sooner than later." I turned my attention to Sleaze and told him to take us on Hurlock. I had a few things that I had to do over there and I can think calmly over there also. Lord knows that I really needed to do some thinking. I don't know if it was anxiety, cancer or that bomb weed but I needed to lax and chill for a few.

CHAPTER 14

"Sleaze, let me use your throwaway phone." He tossed me his phone and I caught it on my way out the backdoor to go see the dogs in the yard. I have 4 pitbulls that I fight(No, I haven't learned shit from the Mike Vick shit). I only have 4 here but I have more at other places. In the yard here I have my special bitch that throws off nothing but winners. Her name is Lady and she's mixed with Red Ape and Termite. I fought her just once and she killed the other dog in 8 minutes. After that kill I only breed her. I do allow her to bump every now & then just to let her release some aggression.

As I enter the yard I call out her name and she jets out of her house wagging her tail wildly with excitement at missing me. It's been a few days since we last saw each other and I'm just as excited to see her. I'm gonna miss her when it's all over for me. I squat down in front of her and she jumps all over me licking my face and whining. "Hey girl!! How's my baby?" I coo into her face.

After receiving all of her joy I stand up and pull my phone out to retrieve Nurse Nakesha's number. When I locate the number I punch it into Sleaze throwaway. She answered her phone saying, "who is this calling me private? And it better be good."

"Well damn, I thought that my reception would be a bit warmer than this," I said in my cool voice.

"Who are you and why do you expect a better reception than this?"

"This is Chips Beautiful," I said.

Within A Week

"Don't be trying to sound all sexy and shit. Who is Chips?"

"I'm guessing that you must give your number to just anybody."

"No I don't. I'm about to hang up. Who is Chips?"

"Baby girl, this is your former patient; Chester."

"Oh my god.... Hey Daddy!! How are you? Are you just now being released?"

"So many questions to answer. I'm fine sweetheart. How're you doing?"

"I'm good baby. I could be better."

"What will make you feel better baby girl?"

"A little TLC."

"TLC? What's TLC? T-Boz, Left Eye and Chili?"

"No silly. Tender Loving Care."

"I thought TLC stood for Thick Long Cock," I said laughing.

"Shit, that'll do too!! I'm glad to hear you laughing."

"I'm just fucking around. I do have the remedy for you though."

"I already know that you have the remedy. The question is when can you give me the remedy?"

"I got you baby girl. I just gotta take care of some things that I couldn't attend to because of my absence. Once I take care of that I'll hit you up and we can get together."

"That's what's up. I'll go get my hair and nails done while I wait for you. I wanna look extra sweet for you."

"You are already extra sweet Beautiful. I'll hit when I'm done."

"Okay Daddy."

After we hung up it dawned on me that I wanted to ask her to check my files at the hospital. Oh well, I'll have to tell her later when I see her. Going back into the house I ran into Black who was carrying a brown paper bag. He said to me, "I'm about to run on the block and hit Gator & Dawg with this bread.."

"Alright lil nigga. Good job earlier. I like how you handled that situation. Come back in about a half. Better yet, hold the block down. We'll come scoop you when we leave here."

"Cool, that's what's up. Thanks for giving me the chance."

"I'll see you in a short lil nigga."

When Black left I locked the door and went into the living room to find Sleaze cleaning and loading up the burners. "How much paper did y'all split from that bag?"

"After choppin out Gator & Dawg 20 bands we both ended up with 65 bands a piece."

"Word? Mike was jive getting it on the low."

"Yeah…. He was holding a grip. I bet this isn't all the bread he had."

"I knew fucking with him was a good move. It's paper in the Fruitbelt."

"Yeah… What's the plan for the evening?" Sleaze asked me.

"I'm not sure yet. Maybe we can go to the Falls or something. Shit, maybe we can put another dick in the dirt."

"You gon crazy bruh!! Because of you four niggaz has been bodied in the last 6 hours."

"I knocked down 3 clowns. Black did Money Mike on his own."

"Yeah, but Black was only there because of you!! You gotta own that body also bruh."

"If that's the case, yo ass got 4 knockdowns too!!"

He pondered that for a second and then said, "I guess I do."

"Anyway, what are you trying to get into tonight?" I asked.

"Let's hit up the strip club and fuck with some stripper hoes."

"That sounds cool but Black ain't old enough to get in."

"The lil nigga will be alright for a little while in the whip. I'll hook the PlayStation up. He'll have that and the computer to keep him company for a little bit."

"Alright, that sounds cool. Let's snatch Black up and grab something to eat. You can drop me off at home afterwards and y'all can come get me around 10 or 11."

CHAPTER 15

While sitting at the table back at the condo Shellz asked Damage, "How long have you been kickin it with Kandy?"

"She's been on my team for years. I got her into this dancing shit."

"She fine as fuck cousin. She'd cake up real lovely in Florida."

"Her competition level wise rose dramatically in Florida. I took her and the twinz there before. Florida has some ice cold bitches!!"

"You took them down there before?"

"Word.. I took them hoes all over."

"You fuck with the twinz too bruh?"

"Them bitches are Kandy's bitches."

"That's pimping for real. Where were you in Florida?"

"I took them to a club in yo city."

"Word? Which club?" Shellz asked.

"We went to that exquisite club called Paradise."

"Say word!! I know where it is. In fact, it's a couple buildings over from where I was going dancing that night I came up on those bricks."

"Probably. I'm not too sure."

"I'm positive. That club has a lot of Italians in it."

"Yep, that's the club," Damage confirmed.

"When was the last time y'all was down there?"

"About 2 years ago I think. Do you remember hearing about a dude found with his fingers cut off and stuffed in his nose?"

"Was he found in an alley or dumpster?"

"Yeah, a dumpster."

"Don't tell me it was you who did that."

"Yeah…… I did that shit."

"No shit? Why? What caused that?"

"It was one of those straight up robberies. We got him for jeweler and cash."

"What was the reason for the fingers in the nose?"

"The fucking Dago wanted a 3some with the twinz and it just so happened that Cream started her period right before he went to eat her pussy. I'm guessing that the Dago smelled period pussy so he put his fingers in his nose symbolizing that he couldn't withstand the odor. Peaches got offended by that and decided to cut his fingers off and stuff them in his nose after Cream shot him through his mouth."

"Damn, them hoes be on it like that bruh?"

"Them bitches are part of my team. They move how I want. My team consists of only bitches."

"Man I was sleeping between 2 beautiful killers."

"Fuck you talking about? They slept with a killer between them at the same time nigga."

"I guess you can say that. We were some sleeping killers," Shellz said smiling.

Kandy strolled into the kitchen with a fat dutch between her fingers. She walked over and kissed Damage on the cheek, said hello to Shellz and said to Damage, "we have a slight problem Daddy. I think I'll have to cancel or change the time for our show tonight and make it for tomorrow."

"Why? What's wrong with tonight? We have plenty of time to get there."

"Getting there in time really isn't the problem."

"Then what is the problem baby girl?"

"Umm… We're supposed to meet Connor for those rocks tonight!!"

"Damn. That shit slipped my mind. Will you be able to switch things?"

"I don't see why not. I really wasn't supposed to perform until tomorrow anyway. Me and the Twinz were only making a special guest appearance anyhow."

"Okay baby, do what needs to be done. We'll head out in the morning."

"Alright Daddy. Here… I rolled this fatty for you. Me and the Twinz are gonna sit in the hot tub. We'll leave in a few hours to go to the club. See you later baby," Kandy said as she kissed him before leaving the room.

Shellz looked at Damage and said, "Yo bitch be on point. I forgot all about the diamond pick-up too."

"Yeah, Kandy be on point with shit. She's mad smart, observant and very observant. That's why I fucks with her as strong as I do."

"She's definitely official."

"Enough of that shit though, let's hit the streets and see what's going on."

CHAPTER 16

Sleaze dropped me off at home and I filled my jacuzzi style bathtub and just sat in it to soak the stress and anguish from within my system. I couldn't believe how my life came tumbling down in a single day. Here it was that I thought of myself as being healthy as a track runner and the next day I have fucking Cancer!! How can this shit be? I felt myself up and I felt healthy and strong. I know that the damn doctors made a mistake somehow. How can a nigga that don't smoke cancer sticks or drink, come down with cancer? I do smoke weed but I don't think weed is cancerous. I know this is some real bullshit!! All of my thinking and the stress within had finally taken its toll and I cried like a baby. I cried hard too. It seemed like I cried for hours but it really was only minutes. After the tears ended I felt refreshed and invigorated. I got out of the tub and walked into my walk-in shower. Several minutes later I found myself standing in front of the vanity mirror looking deep into my eyes searching for my soul. I saw absolutely nothing!! I resigned myself from the mirror and rubbed scented baby oil over myself.

    I walked into my closet and decided to dress casual but comfortable since we were going to the strip club. I put on some loose fit jeans, a wife-beater and a button down shirt with a pair of new Jigga's. I'm not one of those pretty boyz but I allowed my waves to dip hard. I put on a pair of Versace glasses to enhance the look. After assessing myself in the full length mirror I gave my appearance a 2 thumbs up. I went to the kitchen to snack on something. While eating some

Within A Week

fruit my phone buzzed. I recognized the number to be Damage's. After swallowing the bite I had in my mouth I answered with, "Yeah, what up?"

"Chips. It's Damage. What's shakin?"

"Ain't shit really happening. What's good?"

"I'm trying to find out what's good. You got that paper ready?"

"Did you get a call from me yet?" I asked testy.

"Hold up a sec. This is Chips right?"

"Ain't that's who you called?"

"This is Damage Chips, what's with all the slick tongue?"

"I know who this is. This ain't slick tongue talk. I told you that I'd hit you up when I was ready nigga."

"My nigga, you need to pump ya brakes with yo mouth. You are getting way beside yourself with all that slick talk."

This nigga really think he's that nigga. "Nigga please!! I told you that I'd call you when I was ready to hit you with that bread. You should've pumped yo brakes before calling me sweating me about that short paper. That paper is short and bullshit to me."

"Bruh, my bread ain't bullshit. I'm gonna give you a pass for your slick mouth. I'm just gonna blame it on your accident. You must've bumped your head too!!"

"Listen my man; I didn't bump shit. This ain't slick talk either. I'm just telling you what it is. You'll get that paper when I'm ready to give it to you nigga!!"

"Chips who the fuck do you think you talking to? You know how I give it up. Don't make me go there."

"Are you threatening me Damage? I don't take threats too well."

"I'm not threatening you homeboy. I'm just reminding you that I'm about that life being that seems to have forgotten. You shouldn't play yourself like this Chips because you are not ready for what I bring."

"Prove it nigga!! I just chill all the time. I've been ready for anything the streets throw at me. Just to prove it you my nigga, you dead on that paper!! Get it how you live!!"

"Say no more Chips. Buckle up cause it's gonna be a real bumpy ride. I'm gonna kill you sooner than later."

I ended the call and thought to myself, "this nigga really think he's that dude. He must've thought that they stopped making guns after he got his. Something is really wrong with that nigga. He doesn't know it but he chose the right one this time." I smiled to myself forming a thought and called Sleaze. He answered and I said, "I just got off the phone with Damage."

"Yeah? What's up?"

"I deaded that nigga on the bread for the other 10 bricks."

"Word my nigga? Why?"

"I didn't like the way he was talking to me. His mouth was greazy. I felt like he was talking to me like I'm a lil nigga who's supposed to scared of his reputation."

"Oh well, fuck him. It is what it is. He's a dead man walking."

"That's what's up. Snatch up Black and meet me at my spot on Herman. Be ready cause we're going to the strip club from there."

"If I see Damage anywhere in traffic can I light his ass up?"

"I would give you the green light on his ass but I want him for delf. Just be on point and don't let him get the drop on you."

"Alright. I'll hit you when I get Black."

"Do that bruh," I said as I disconnected the line. I took another bite of my apple and thought how fortunate I was to have Sleaze as my right hand. I truly hope he survives this bullshit God threw at me and I threw at him.

I went to my room and grabbed 2 pistols with extended clips and a few stacks to blow at the club. I snatched my keys off the dresser and set the alarm on the building as I bounded out the house. On my ride to Herman I was trying to entertain good thoughts concerning good things. I'm sure that the way my life was unravelling that good thoughts only existed in my head.

* * * * *

Within A Week

Damage was up pacing back & forth. He was heated to say the least. He said, "I can't believe this nigga. This nigga not even built like that. Yet he had the audacity to come at me crooked like he did. He had to bump his head in that accident he was in."

"Who are you talking about kinfolk?"

"I'm talking about that bitch-ass nigga chips!!"

"That's the nigga you gave them bricks to right? I thought y'all were cool cousin?" Shellz asked.

"We were cool. That fool lost his mind a few minutes ago when I called about that bread. When I see his dumb ass I'm gonna make sure he lose his mind!!"

"What happened? What did he say bruh?"

"The punk nigga told me that I'm dead on that bread for them other 10 bricks. Then the fuck-boy had the nerves to tell me in so many words that we at war."

"I thought he was cool cuz? What could've happened to cause this?"

"I don't know what is going on and I don't even give a fuck either. That nigga violated and he's gonna pay for his violations with his life!! Don't sweat that paper for those bricks cousin, I'll give you the bread myself. I'm really tight right now. Talking like he did was one thing but to blatantly tell me that he's walking me for that bread only added fuel to the fire!! I'm gonna knock his head off!! On everything I love!!"

"Cool out some cuz. You gotta have a cool head. The nigga is on the radar and we'll put his dick in the dirt. Right now we gotta focus on getting them diamonds."

"You're right. Chips is already dead. We gotta get those diamonds." Damage was still hot about everything when he yelled, "Kandy!! You bitches ready?"

Kandy yelled back from upstairs, "Damn Daddy, why do we gotta be bitches?"

"Not now Kandy. Y'all need to get the fuck up out of here and get to the club so y'all can wait on dude with the diamonds."

"Alright Daddy, we're leaving in a few minutes."

"Good, We'll be there in a few hours. If Connor get there before we do make sure he drops them stones. Make sure you hit me on the hip as soon as you see him. Prolong your visit seeing him."

"Okay Daddy. I'll call you later. I love you."

"I love you more."

Damage turned his attention back to Shellz and said, "c'mon cuz, let's roam the streets and see if we can run into that nigga Chips. If I see him it's blast on sight!! I don't give a fuck who's he with or where he's at… it's see him metal spray!!"

"Let's roll."

CHAPTER 17

"It doesn't look like that dude Sleaze is out here. We probably shouldn't circle the block again. It looks like some of them lil niggaz is being weary," Shellz said to Damage.

"Yeah… I see them lil niggaz with hands close to their waist. Let's keep it moving. Lucky Chips bitch-ass ain't out here, I was gonna hit him up regardless."

"We would've been in a big gun fight too. It's about 15 of them lil niggaz out there and at least 14 is holding."

"You're probably right too. The way I feel right now I wouldn't have given a fuck. That nigga is so deep under my skin right now that I wouldn't be able to contain that pressure if I saw his ass anywhere. Let's hit a bar for a few drinks so I can take the edge off."

* * * * *

"Anyway Black, I'm sure that Sleaze done told you but I still gotta tell you myself. Riding with me right now you'll be putting yourself in all types of danger. You're subjecting yourself to an early death and/or in jail forever. It's totally up to you if you back out or roll. I won't have any hard feelings if you choose to walk away. If you choose to stay I'd expect you to move how I say move, bang when I say bang and aim to kill not wound. The call is yours lil nigga."

Man Chips, I've been waiting on this for a long time. Count me all the way in. I mean that shit literally!! Count me in prison, a casket or living lavish!! Whatever is the outcome I'm trying to see it to i's end."

"Cool. Check this out though, we're going to the strip club right now and you're not old enough to get in. You can come for the ride or we can come scoop you afterwards," Sleaze told Black.

"I'm cool with sitting in the car playing the game. I wanna be around in case y'all come up some pussy or some bird-ass niggaz looking to die."

"You sure lil nigga?" I asked.

"Yeah. Go do y'all. I'll be good."

Several minutes later we pulled into the clubs parking area. It wasn't jammed pack but it appeared to be a decent enough number of people there. The bouncer at the door was a nigga I knew. We weren't tight but we were cool enough. So I slipped him 2 hundred dollar bills so he'd ignore searching us. The inside of the club was stylishly put together. There was a huge stage for the feature girl and it was surrounded with smaller stages for patrons to get private but not personal dances. Against the far wall was a bar area that extended from the front to the back of the club. There was even a short order cook for the hungry. The house specialty was of course Buffalo Wings. It was cool how they had the DJ's booth higher than the stage but right behind it. The DJ was spinning nothing but ass shaking music.

We found a booth that placed our backs against the wall and a clear view of the door. After sitting down, a sexy white Monkey came over to take our orders. I don't drink but Sleaze likes to sip on a Corona. We ordered 40 wings and a Corona for him and a bottled water for me. As the waitress turned to leave I saw that she had a PHAT ASS!! Where are these white bitches getting all this ass from? I had to stop her in her tracks and get in her business a bit. I put on my bitch-getter smile & charm and said, "excuse me Beautiful, I don't mean to hold you up from your job but what is your name?"

She smiled back and said, "I'm Chythia but I'm called Cynt."

"What a lovely smell... I mean name. I'm Chips," I said as I stuck my hand out to shake hers. She placed her soft and delicate hands

Within A Week

in mine as we stared into each others eyes. Her flushed cheeks told me that I got deeper than the flesh. She softly let her hand fall from mine as she turned away and added a little more sway in her walk. I looked at Sleaze and said, "I got her bruh. She's the one!!"

"The one? As in wifey?"

"Hell nah fool. The one for tonight or maybe tomorrow night," I laughed. "Don't forget fool, I only have a few more days on this earth."

"Man…. You gon live forever!! You better get her credentials before we get up out of here."

"She's all mine. I'm that nigga."

Cynt came back with our drinks and gave me the bill. On the back of the bill was her phone number. I placed the number in my pocket and gave her a C-Note with my phone number on it and told her to keep the change. She left and came back a few minutes later carrying a huge smile and our wings. Sleaze dug into them wings like he was in competition. I had no choice but to join in or not eat. I dove in just like Sleaze did. After we dusted the wings I liked my fingers and sat back to check out some hoes. I was just laxing when Sleaze tapped me on the shoulder and pointed with his head in the direction he wanted my attention. I looked in that direction and saw another thick ass white bitch. This one right here was dope ass fuck!! She wasn't just thick, she was extremely beautiful too.

Before I go further let's be clear; I honor, cherish and love my beautiful black Queens!! Can't another race of women make me desert my sisters. I'm dying soon so fuck it… I'll dip in some vanila.

Anyway, this white girl was like a sculpture. She was flawless as far as her physical attributes went. Her clear flaw to me was her choice of occupation. Sleaze got her attention and called her over. Her walk said that she carried some bomb ass pussy in her thongs!! When she got to us she said, "what up sexy?"

Sleaze went right in, "hey Gorgeous, how are you? What's your name?"

"I'm fine. My name is Peaches. How are you guys doing?"

"You damn right you're fine. I'm Sleaze and this my bruh, Chips."

"Nice to meet y'all. Haven't seen you guys here before."
"This our first time. We're not the strip club type."
"What bring y'all here tonight?" Peaches asked.
"You!!"
She smiled and said, "whatever smooth talker."
"We were just chillin and heard about the wings here."
"The wings huh?"
"And the women. Can't forget the women."
"You're funny!! Do you want a private dance Sleaze?"
"Do bitches sit down to pee? Hell yeah I wanna feel that booty!!"
She grabbed his hand and headed further to the back of the club. While Sleaze was gone I hit Black on the chirp phone to check on him. "What up lil homie, you good?"
"Yea, no doubt. I'm chillin as usual."
"I'm about to order you some wings and have one the waitresses bring it out to you so be listening for my beep."
"Alright big homie, I'll be listening for it. Good looking!!"
No sooner than I disconnected with Black that Monkey Peaches came strutted over wearing a different get up and without my nigga Sleaze. She licked her lips like she actually ate the nigga up and said, "damn Daddy, you fine as fuck!! What's your name?"
I laughed and said, "funny!! Where's my lil brother?"
"Your brother? Who is your brother?"
"I already said it's funny. Now where is my brother?"
She looked at me with certain bewilderment in her eyes like she had the slightest idea what I was talking about. She said, "I really have the slightest idea what you're talking about. I never met anyone named Sleaves."
"It's Sleaze!! Bitch you better stop playing with me before I shut this club the fuck down."
Just as I said that I saw Sleaze coming from the back with the biggest grin on his face. Coming behind him that bitch Peaches…. Again!! My mind started doing all kinds of flips. How can that bitch be here & there? I guess the symptoms of my cancer are starting to kick in or that Pineapple shit is good as fuck!! I knew that I wasn't

Within A Week

tripping because when Sleaze looked and saw Peaches standing in front of me he looked behind him and saw Peaches there also. The one in front of me seen the confusion and smirked before she said, "that must be your brother Sleaves."

"Sleaze," I corrected her.

"Well, your brother is in front of you. From the smile on his face he must've experienced one of my sisters private shows. I'm Cream and that's my twin sister Peaches."

I extended my hand and gently shook her hand. I was mesmerized by these bad bitches. I was wondering where they came from. I've never seen 3 thick ass and fine ass white bitches in one setting before. I really must have Cancer!! I came outta my trance and said, "I'm Chips. It's nice to meet you Cream."

She took in my state of confusion to attack with her chance to get some bread outta me by saying, "would you like a private dance?"

"No thanks. I'm good."

Sleaze intercepted the offer and said, "I'll take his!!" Just like Peaches did earlier, Cream grabbed his hand and led him to the back.

Peaches was just standing there awkwardly for a few seconds until I invited her to have a seat. I offered her a drink, which she declined and asked me, "are you always this quiet & shy?"

"I'm never shy... Always quiet!!"

She smiled and said, "when you do talk you still don't say much. Do you not like me Chips?"

"You cool sweetheart. You and your sister are some really bad bitches. I'm just not really a strip club type of nigga."

"Oh.. I understand."

Just as she was finna get up and leave she was hugged from behind by an Ice Cold Black Monkey. This Monkey was fabulous!! I was staring at her with wide eyes and a slack jawed. The black beauty said to Peaches, "Hey sexy, who is this fine ass nigga you chatting with?"

"Girl, this is Chips."

The black girl said, "Hey sexy, I'm Kandy. How are you?"

"I'm good Kandy. Thanks. Are you sweet as your name?"

"Sweeter sweetheart!!"

"I would think so….. What's the flavor?"

She laughed and replied, "would you like to taste for yourself and determine the flavor on your own?"

I shook my head yeah and smiled my smile. Kandy looked over to Peaches and sent her to get Cynt. Cynt appeared in seconds with her phat ass and dazzling smile. She said, "what's up Kandy?"

"This fine ass nigga here wanted to see how I taste."

Cynt smiled, licked her lips and strolled over to me and put her tongue in my mouth. After the kiss Kandy said, "what flavor do I taste like?"

I smiled again and licked my lips. Cynt bent down to my ear and said, "I want you to taste me at the same time I taste you. Hopefully I'll see you around 3 or 3:30 am."

I nodded it was on and I slapped her on her phat ass. Kandy & Peaches hugged each other and walked towards Cream as Sleaze came to the booth with a bigger smile than the first time. He said, "bruh, these bitches are fine. I got both of their numbers. I'm trying to hook up with both of them!!"

"That's what's up."

"Who was that badd bitch they dipped off with?"

"Her name is Kandy. She is the coldest!!"

"What's up with her?"

"She's probably just like them white hoes!! I did taste her pussy though!!"

"For real? How?" Sleaze asked amazed.

"She must've let the waitress bitch eat her pussy because I asked what flavor she taste like and she had the waitress bitch come and put her tongue in my mouth!!"

"Man, I hope she's just like the white bitches because I wanna fuck her!!"

"I ordered some wings for Black but they're taking forever to get to him. Let's get up out of here so he can eat something before we go hunting."

CHAPTER 18

Connor was in a hurry to get this day over with. Throughout the day he's been grouchy and on edge. His wife noticed his behavior and showed concern for him. "Honey, is there something wrong?" She asked him when they were in the store alone.

"No sweetie, I'm just tired is all."

"You should be tired, you've barely slept. Hell, I've barely slept."

"I'm sorry for that sweetheart."

"Don't worry yourself with that. We'll be alright," she chided.

It wasn't that Connor was really tired, he was more concerned with how he was gonna get his hands on the needed diamonds without his wife finding out. He was devising and dismissing plans all day long. He began to stress even harder until his wife said, "don't forget that I have a hair appointment this evening."

Relief flooded his body as he remembered that he'll be closing the store himself. "I remember honey," he said as he looked at his watch.

"It's almost 4 now and I'll be leaving in a few."

"Okay sweetie, I got things under control. You can go ahead and get there early. I'll close up at 5 exactly."

His wife left and left Connor alone to do his thing. At 5 o'clock on the dot Connor shut things down and rushed out of the store and secured it tight. He had a black pouch in his jacket pocket that contained the $200 thousand dollars of diamonds. Jumping into his luxury car he rushed home to shower and change from the clothes that he's been sweating in all day. He dressed quickly so that he could be out of the house before his wife got there.

Connor zoomed to the strip club to handle this business because he really didn't have any intentions of staying long. He just wanted to drop off the jewels and be done with the whole ordeal. Connor parked in the back right next to my whip but didn't notice the young black man sitting in the car next to him. The young black man did notice Connor and his every move. Connor removed himself from the car and pulled out the black pouch that contained the diamonds to recheck it and then put them back in his jacket pocket. Connor then phoned Kandy to inform her that he'll be inside shortly. At the same time that Connor was on the phone with Kandy Black had hit me on the chirp. I got the chirp as Sleaze and I was about to leave. Black said, "Chips, it's a lick out here. It's a white dude with mad diamonds in his jacket."

"Stop playing lil nigga."

"Real talk bruh."

"Where is he at right now?"

"He's heading right there."

"Follow him so we can sandwich him in."

"I'm moving now. Come on."

Connor was completely oblivious to being stalked. As soon as he rounded the corner we bumped into each other. Connor was a bit startled and immediately started apologizing, "I'm sorry fellas. Are you alright?"

"Don't worry about it. We'll be good."

Sleaze chimed in with, "yeah, no doubt."

Black came from behind Connor and put him in a major choke hold. As Connor was being hemmed up I reached in Connors inside pockets and pulled out a black pouch that Black said was there. Sleaze told Black to release him. Before Black released him I grabbed the white dude by the hair and told Black to leave being that his face was never seen. Sleaze got right in the white dudes face and said, "We see each other and you know how we look but you don't know how my other partner looks. If the police come for either one of us

Within A Week

our other partner will find you and kill everything in the house; including the fish if you have any!!"

The white dude just look in the sky and said, "what the fuck?! This is a terrible week!!"

When Connor hadn't made it inside soon enough Kandy came outside to find Conner leaning against the wall breathing heavy and face flushed red as a cooked lobster. She rushed to Connor and asked, "what happened? Are you alright? Why are you looking like that?"

Connor let tears escape his eyes as he said, "NO I'm not alright!! Ever since I got you alone my life has been Shitty!! I had to steal my own jewels from my family and then I fucking get robbed for them."

"Who did this?"

"Three fucking nigg.... Black dudes. I rounded the corner here and crashed into 2 of them as the third one came from behind and choked me."

"How did they look?" Kandy asked hoping that Damage did it.

"I only saw the guy with the glasses clearly."

Kandy started to describe Damage but remembered I just left. She described me to Connor and he confirmed that it was indeed me.

When Connor had called Kandy to say that he'll be in there in a minute; she had called Damage and learned that Damage was already on his way there. Several miles away Damage and Chips passed each other going in opposite directions. Damage saw Chips and was about to give chase but his phone rang again and it was Kandy. He answered, "what?"

"Hurry and get here. Some niggaz just robbed Connor for our rocks."

Damage thought that he should pursue Chips but his mind told him that those rocks were more important than his personal beef. Besides, he would've gotten his head knocked off had he chosen differently.

Arriving at the club, Damage hopped out and was crowded by Kandy, Peaches & Cream. Kandy said, "Daddy, I think these 2 dudes that were here earlier robbed Connor for the rocks."

"Two dudes? How'd they look?"

"I know their names. One of them got dances from Peaches and Cream."

Damage already who it was and said, "Chips and Sleaze?"

"Yeah... That's them... Who are they?"

"A coupla dead niggaz. Tell Connor not to call the police and to just go home and we'll get in touch with him at another time."

As I'm admiring the stones my ring. It's Damage, "you really think you tough huh Chips?"

"Is this a repeat conversation? If so, I heard it already!!"

"Listen Chips, I'm willing to let that other shit ride if you just come back to the club and give me back my rocks!!"

"Your rocks? I don't have your rocks."

"Yo bitch-ass just robbed my white boy for my Diamonds. Just give my Diamonds up."

"To be absolutely honest Damage, I did just rob a white boy for some Diamonds. The only thing is, The Diamonds I robbed are My Diamonds!!" I hung up on him and threw that phone out the window. Sleaze was looking at me with wonder in his eyes and asked, "what was that all about?"

"That was Damage and he said that the diamonds we got are his."

"How did he know to contact you?"

"I would say one of them bitches. I saw that fine as black bitch helping that cracker as we dipped outta there. So I'm gonna guess that the Kandy broad is Damage bitch and she was waiting for the white boy to get there with the stones."

"You're probably right too," Sleaze said matter of factly.

"I'm sure of it bruh. I'm glad that we came here. We got some Diamonds and we fucked Damage again!!"

CHAPTER 19

Back at Kandy's condo Damage was sitting at the kitchen table with Shellz and the girls around him. He said furiously to the whole table, "I want that niggaz head!! On everything I love he's a dead nigga!!"

"Daddy try to relax. You think best under a cool head. You don't move to the best of your abilities upset."

"You're right Kandy." He looked at the twinz and asked, "did any of you bitches get any numbers on them?"

"No, but the Sleaze dude has my number," Cream said to Damage.

"He has mine also," said Peaches.

"Both of you bitches gave the same nigga y'all number? What type of bonehead shit is that?"

Peaches said, "he tipped well and I saw him as a potential vic. I didn't know that Cream gave her number too!!"

Cream said, "yeah, he gave me $200 just to lick my clit."

"Mine too!! He said that he wants to spend some money tomorrow."

"That's what's up. That whole Cleveland thing is done for until further notice. When that nigga Sleaze call one of y'all I want you to set it up for some night of fucking. Shellz and I will figure the set-up and I want either one of you bitches to make sure that he comes to y'all."

* * * * *

"Hello?" I answered.
"Hi… Is this Chips?" Asked a unfamiliar voice.
"Yeah, who dis?"
"This is Cynt."
"Cynt?"
"From the strip club."
"Oh yeah, what's up gorgeous?"
"You!!"
"Oh yeah?"
"Definitely you!! I'm trying to see you daddy. Remember what I whispered in your ear?"
"How can I forget? Where are you right now?"
"In the clubs parking lot."
"Alright, come to the east side."
"Where on the east side?":
"Come to Box off of Moselle."
"Box n Moe? You from over there? We can't we meet somewhere?"
"Trust me baby. You'll be good. Call me when you get to Genesee and Moselle."
"Have your phone on hand daddy, I don't wanna be out there by myself."
"I got you baby girl, just come on."

We were at my spot on Herman. I gave Black the keys to my Intrepid and sent him on the block to wait for Cynt. I wasn't too sure if she was attached to Damage so I had to play careful. Before Black left I said, "make sure that she leaves her purse and phone in the car. Have her park her car on French in Hummers garage and bring her to me on Main street off of Bailey. Take side streets to get there so you can see the follower if there is one. If there is one push her wig bag."

"Alright big homie, I got you. Anything else?"

"Nah, just stay on point. After you drop her off you can go home and get some rest."

"Ok cool."

I turned to Sleaze and said, "don't call any of them other hoes. Keep yoor phones on and stay on point. Follow the rules of war."

Within A Week

"Alright bruh. You be safe and I'll see you in the morning."
"Early my nigga."
"No doubt."

* * * * *

Fifteen minutes later my phone rang, "Speak on it," I said when I saw it was Cynt.

"Hey Daddy I'm on Genesee about to turn on Moselle."

"Alright, come down to Box and pull up behind the black Intrepid. My lil brother is in the car and he'll give you his phone and I'll be talking to you from there."

"What's with that? Should I just hook up with you at another time?"

"Nah sexy, it's all good. My brother is there for your safety."

Twenty seconds later Black hit me up, "Chips, shorty is here. Damn OG you tell me how fine she is or how phat that ass is!!"

"Relax lil homie, I'll try to hook you with her soon enough."

"That's what I'm talking about. Here she is."

After Black parked her car and she got in with him he used side streets to meet up with me at Shoshones swimming pool. Cynt hopped out the Intrepid with the biggest smile when she saw me. After sitting that juicy ass on my leather she said, "Whew, I was scared for a second."

"Scared? Of what?"

"Well, your brother looks so serious. Not to mention that he had this big gun sitting on his lap."

"My lil bro is good money. He had that gun to protect yo fine ass."

"Protect me from who?"

"Nobody in particular but my block is crazy like you said. I just wanted you to be safe and feel safe."

"I'm cool now. Are you carrying also?"

"The street term is holding, strapped or packing; yeah... I'm good."

"So where are we going daddy?"

"You'll know when we get there," I said as I pumped Camron and Lil Wayne's old joint Suck it or Not.

Cynt listened to the lyrics and said, "Really?"

I smiled my smile and said, "Suck it or Not."

She smiled, leaned over and unzipped my jeans pulled out my dick and sucked me all the way to our destination.

CHAPTER 20

I got up a few hours later after laying pipe to Cynt fine ass. I called Black to meet me so that he can take her back to her car. I'm not too keen on white girls but Cynt was an alright bitch. Her head game was really close to perfect!! She had a nice deepthroat and sucked deeply with a sloppy mouth. The topping was she wanted a nigga to jerk off into her mouth so her face can be sloppy and she swallows whatever lands in her mouth. My type of freak bitch. I didn't mention the pussy!! That was A-1 also. She can take dick and work those pussy muscles. When I hit it from the back it was delightful watching her fat ass wiggle and jiggle. She loved when I pushed my thumb in her ass in that position. She was definitely worth chillin with. Perhaps I'll get up with her again sooner than later. It'll have to be sooner because according to the doctors I'll be dead later.

Anyway, after she got in the car with Black I called Sleaze and had him meet me on Herman. Twenty minutes later he came through with some breakfast from McDonalds. Is it just me or do Mickey D's have some good pancakes? While we ate I asked him about my dopefiend father. "I haven't seen him since he cleaned the kennels," Sleaze told me.

"That's unusual isn't it? No matter how I feel about him he'd still come by begging for shit."

"Yeah… He should've come by already. Maybe he did and we weren't there."

"Maybe," I said, taking a sip of juice. "Anyway, I'm going to chill with that nurse chick for a while. If anything pops up you know how to reach me. Before I hook up with girly though I wanna go by a few dope spots to see if my father was seen."

We hopped in Sleaze whip and headed to Montana. At the store on Genny and Moe we saw Gator & Dawg going inside. Sleaze beeped at them and we all raised the peace sign. We continued on and turned left on Montana. Halfway down the block we pulled up in front of a player friend of mine named Chucky. Chucky's a good nigga. We go back to grade school. We played ball together. I was shooting guard and he ran point. We were tearing shit up. Together we were called Nice & Smooth!! We won multiple championships together.

If he wasn't playing ball he was selling dope in school. The white kids were stealing money from their parents just to give it Chucky. The school money wasn't enough because he quit school and pounded the block all day with that dope. Our friendship lasted throughout our different directions in life at that time. When I jumped into the drug game it was Chucky who put me on. I called his number from outside his building and he answered with, "Chips, You came to fuck with me again or are you already rich?"

I laughed and said, "Chucky, I will always fuck with you. I'm not rich though."

"I know that's right. What's good though my dude?"

"I'm wondering if my pops have been through here or if anybody has seen him."

"I hope we don't have a problem if he was."

"Nah my nigga. My pops grown as hell. He's gonna do whatever he wants, if I like it or not. I'm asking because I haven't seen him in a few and I'd usually see his begging ass more often than not."

"Oh… I hear you on that. I'm on my way outside. I see y'all out there. I'll call Tre' on my way out and ask him if he's seen your pops."

Chucky looked the same as usual. Money agrees with him. It was barely 9am and he was looking like a million bucks. He sported

Within A Week

a low-cut skin fade. He had on a pair of throwback Jordan's with the wings on them. His jewels was gleaming and icy as fuck. With his appearance screaming money, he was the same ole nigga that I knew from way before. He embraced me and said, "Chips my nigga... You still got that killer crossover and jumpshot?"

"Hell yeah nigga. What did you think?" I questioned as I imitated my crossover and jumpshot. "I'd lose a liver before I lose my jumpshot!!"

We dapped again and kicked it for a few as we awaited his lil homie Tre' call back. When his phone rang he looked at the ID and said, "This him now, hold up." When he got off the phone he said to me, "the last he saw your pops your pops was laid out on a stretcher on Ferry & Goodyear."

"What do you mean laid out on a stretcher? What happened?"

"He was hopping up the street and got hit by one of those delivery vans. The ambulance came and scooped him up."

"For real my nigga? Did Tre' say this happened?"

"He said about 2 maybe 3 days."

"Damn... Thanks my nigga. I appreciate it."

"Anything. Anytime Chips. I hope he's alright."

"Thanks again bruh. Be easy out here. There's a lot of suckas roaming the streets."

"You don't have to tell me twice."

I hopped back in the car and we sped off. I was quiet for a second trying to rationalize what I've just heard. Sleaze turned the beats down and asked, "Is everything cool bruh? You look down."

"Yeah.. I mean, nah. He told me that my pops got hit by a van a couple days ago."

"For real? I just saw his ass a couple days ago. I haven't heard anything on the streets."

"This must've happened after you saw him."

"What's the move?"

"I don't know yet. Let's go back on Herman. Call Black and tell him to hug the block until I call him."

While Sleaze was calling Black I was calling Nurse Nakesha. She answered with a beautiful voice after stretching, "good morning handsome!! I was hoping to hear from you last night. I'm a patient girl though."

"Sorry about that Beautiful. My intention was to come chill with you but some bullshit came up."

"I understand. So what's going on this morning? I hope it's what I want to be up."

"Damn baby girl, you're about to wake the sleeping giant. Especially if you keep on using that sexy ass bedroom voice of yours."

"Well, I'm in my bedroom. All alone and naked!!"

"How sexy that sight must be. Wish I was there to take it in."

"I wish you could be here also. So what's going on this morning baby?"

"Sweetheart, my pops was admitted to the hospital due to an accident."

"Sorry to hear that. Is he alright?"

"That; is what I don't know and need to find out."

"What would you like for me to do?"

"Would you be able to call and see if he was admitted there and released?"

"Yeah, I can do that for you. What's your father's name?"

"Same as mine. Chester Chambers."

"What day did his accident occur?"

"Two maybe three days ago."

"Alright Daddy. Call me back later and I'll have the information for you."

"Alright sweetheart. Thank you. You're an Angel."

"Yeah, yeah nigga. Whatever," she said jokingly.

"Seriously baby girl. When I hit you up later it's for you to come through."

"Alright baby. See you later."

Sleaze dropped me off on Herman. I went inside and stretched out on the living room sofa. That's where I eventually fell asleep and slept well. It was the best sleep I had in my life….. At least that's what it felt like. It only lasted three hours though. I was awakened by a steady pounding on my door and the ringing of my phone. I looked at the time and it read 1:20pm. I grabbed my burner from the end table and answered my phone on the way to the door.

CHAPTER 21

"Sleaze, what's up?" I said into the phone.

"I'm at the door; open up nigga."

When I opened the door, Sleaze burst in breathing heavily. He had a look in his eyes that represented death. He was sweating profusely like a faucet was left on. I closed the door behind him and asked, "Damn bruh, you look like hell!! What's going on?"

"Man, some of them Fruitbelt niggaz came thru on some bullshit. We was just bangin with them niggaz on the block."

"Say word!!"

"Word bruh. Shit was wild out there."

"Fuck!! Tell me what happened."

"We were all on the block shooting dice. It was some big paper out there too!! Them niggaz from the other end of Box was out there stopping everything!! That nigga from GYC had came thru too. There was so much bread out there that Gator & Dawg was out there shooting they shot."

"So what the hell happened?"

"A brown Blazer came thru asking about you. Of course when they spoke of you Gator & Dawg asked them why. One of the dudes said some slick shit and you already know how Dawg gives it up. He told them niggaz to raise up before they get raised up. One of the niggaz from the backseat lowered his window and showed a K-Cutter."

"That was a stupid mistake. What was he thinking?"

Within A Week

"I don't know what that clown was thinking. All I know is that he shouldn't have done it."

"What happened bruh?" I asked anxiously.

"You already know how the block is always flooded with mad shooters Black and Lil Pop stood on the side of Dawg. When they saw the window coming down they already had their burners out and in the clutch. When the tip of that K-Cutter was revealed Black & Pop let them bullets fly. The driver hit the gas and tried to get the hell out of there but he didn't get too far. Out of nowhere the niggaz Ty, Pull, Frog and Smash came out bangin on the Blazer. They ripped that Blazer into little pieces. The 3 niggaz that was inside had found God because they was Holy!!" Sleaze laughed at his humor.

"Okay... One more question."

"What's that?"

"You never mentioned yourself in anything, why are you looking all confused and sweaty?"

"I'm sweating because themlil niggaz don't aim. They just start dumping in a certain direction. It had to be at least 70 rounds scattered everywhere."

"Okay, why do you look confused?"

"Cause I was out here bangin on your door and calling your phone. You took forever to answer either one. I was kinda worried that them niggaz was a diversion and you was the real target. I was worried about you."

"Aw... How sweet!! You Ralph Trasvant ass nigga!!"

"Fuck you nigga... Ain't nothing sensitive about me."

"Whatever bruh. Where's Black? Everything cool around the way?"

"Black is on Hurlock chillin. The block is flooded with all shades of devils doing what they do. Gator & Dawg bounced to Lockport while everyone else went their own way."

"Hit Black up and tell him that we're gonna right on them Fruitbelt niggaz. Them niggaz wanna come looking for me? I'm gonna bring myself to them. Tell Black to put on his vest and gat fully loaded. I want you to go grab him and come back here. I'm gonna go and snatch up some more artillery."

"Hell yeah Chips, that's what I'm talking about. I love this Chips right here. Let's right on them fools."

"We're about to."

CHAPTER 22

"Damn, what the fuck happened over here?" Shellz asked.

"I have the slightest idea!! Shit looks mad wild out here. Niggaz must've been at war," Damage replied.

"Had too. All types of officials out here. It's even a coupla Coroners vans too."

"Hell yeah!!"

Shellz got a good idea what type of niggaz my niggaz is as he said, "These niggaz be wild'n huh man?"

"Welcome to Ruff Buff!!"

Damage was on his own little mission to get my life. Him coming thru at that time was pure coincidence. He's not tight to the Fruitbelt. He also didn't know that my lil niggaz was on the lookout for him. The order wasn't to kill him though. I just wanted a word if he's seen. Damage was all mine for delf. Sleaze can't get at him unless it's life or death situations.

* * * * *

Without me knowing, Frog was with Black & Sleaze when they arrived back. I wasn't too sure if Frog was ready for the havoc that I was ready to bring but it was cool with me that he was there. By all means, the lil nigga just participated in a multiple homi. Frog stood before me and said, "What's up Chips, you heard about that work I just put in on the block?"

"Yeah lil nigga, I just heard about it. That was some real nigga shit. I respect y'all lil niggaz for the courage y'all show and being official as a referees whistle. Before I fully accept you coming along with us I need you to know that there's a great chance we die on the streets young or in jail old."

"I'm down to ride OG. Your enemy is my enemy. Prison won't come though because I'm down to hold court in the streets."

I embraced the lil nigga and welcomed him to catch a few bodies.

Let me give you a rundown on who Frog is. His real name is Cordero Jackson. He is the cousin of a real nigga I grew up with named Eazy Erik. Erik is a member of Box n Moe whose doing 30 years in prison. If he makes it out of there he'll be immediately admitted to a crazy house!! Eazy killed a rat nigga from Delavan during a shootout in-which Eazy's lil sister Tisha got killed. Seeing his baby sister go down caused Eazy to lose his mind. He killed the shooter of his sister in broad daylight; right in front of this devil FBI agent.

Anyway, back to Frog; he's a real live-wire. You should have an idea from his exploits earlier. He was a real lil nigga when his cousin Tisha got killed. He was actually playing with her during that shootout. Perhaps that incident plays a part in Frog's life. He barely was allowed to stay a full day in school. He was eventually kicked out of 7th grade for bringing a gun to school and pulling out on the Principal. Since his childhood he's been brought home numerous times by the police for all types of disturbances. What I'm about to share with you is something I learned from Gator. I was told that Frog learned the location of some of the niggaz that was involved with Tisha's death and walked over to their block and took revenge. Dawg was on the same bullshit that Frog was on and accompanied the lil nigga. They knocked off three niggaz that day and since then Frog has been close to Gator & Dawg.

* * * * *

I gave my niggaz the rundown on how I want shit to go. "Alright y'all, check how we're going to do this shit; we're gonna go through

Within A Week

there in 2 waves. The first wave will be precise shooting. I want leg shots or body shots just to stop niggaz from running away. The second wave will kill any and everybody left breathing. After we execute that little business we're gonna go over to Big Rob's house and wait for his bitch-ass come out."

"Who is Big Rob?" Black asked.

"Big Rob is the head nigga from over there. He's their shot-caller. He's the one who sent them niggaz on the block. The bread we took from Money Mike was his bread. He gotta die today!! If niggaz came and sprayed ya block up would you come out?"

"You muthafuckin right I'm coming out," Black stated.

"Exactly!!"

We sat on Herman blazing that Pineapple Express shit while we cleaned, oiled and loaded our weapons. We had only a few handguns. They were for the Big Rob job. We were all using assault rifles and shotguns. After every gun was completed I addressed everyone, "Sleaze, I want you in the second wave. I'm gonna right in the first wave with Black. I'm gonna have Black pick off those crazy muthafuckaz Body & Soul. Them 2 niggaz have no regard for life. They are real official with their murder game. We'll have to knock them off first. Y'all come behind us 30 seconds later and use the grenade launcher and make that shit look like a scene from a war movie in Iraq."

That excited Sleaze. He said, "Hell yeah my nigga. I'm gonna love letting off one of those bombs!! I'm gonna knock everything off with that bitch!!" Sleaze smiled.

"What about me?" Frog asked.

"On this one you're gonna drive."

"All man…. I wanna push some heads back too."

"You will lil homie. You and Black can push Big Rob's wig into a weave. He doesn't know who y'all is and seeing y'all won't cause him to be prepared for war. Y'all can empty the 16 rounds in y'all burners into his face if y'all like."

"Alright bet!!" Frog said with some happiness.

I smiled at him and said, "I'm glad to see that you're happy now. Now pass that L."

CHAPTER 23

We left my spot headed to the Fruitbelt with 2 whips full of weapons. We took the simplest route there. I'm sure that if we tried to sneak in that we'd be spotted more easily and reported. We got on the highway and got off at Goodell and turned down Michigan street to High street and saw them niggaz just chillin on the corner. Sleaze and Frog stayed back on Michigan and listened through the chirp phone. I said to Black, "Body & Soul are the 2 niggaz with the black gloves on. I'm gonna give them a burst from the SK and spray up anybody near them. Drive real slow so that I make sure that them niggaz are out of work."

"The 2 niggaz with the braids?" Black asked.

"Yeah… That's them."

"Got it. Ready?"

"Let's ride my nigga."

Black started driving while I lowered the window and hung out that bitch with the SK at the ready. The first burst of fire hit Body & Soul in the legs. Then I switched it to fully auto and spraying shit like windex on a window. Niggaz tried to turn the block into a track meet and run for safety. But there was no safety to be had. I swept the SK into a line from side to side. Bullets were flying everywhere and hitting everything in its path. Most of the niggaz that tried to run got hit in the back. Some dove behind trees and cars trying to hide. I let off about 20 more rounds before Black stepped on the gas. I spoke into the chirp that it was Sleaze turn to do his thing. Frog bent the

Within A Week

corner and Sleaze hung out of his window with the M-16 ready to sound off. Sleaze noticed that a few niggaz came to assist the fallen soldiers and he aimed at them and let off a grenade into the area. We were about 4 blocks ahead of them but I felt the ground tremble. I looked back and saw bodies and body parts flying in the air from the impact. The explosion filled the sky like a scene from a hollywood movie. Seconds later I heard the rapid fire of Sleazes M-16. I was in awe watching this shit. It's not in many people's lifetime that you'd be able to participate or even witness anything like this. The shit you see on TV is exactly that; TV. It's nothing like seeing this shit first hand. I saw the slaughter, I heard the screams and I can only imagine the carnage that was left behind. The most fucked up shit was that Sleaze was laughing during it all and I was happy for the enjoyment he was receiving.

After leaving the Fruitbelt we went straight to Grey street where I knew Big Rob would be. Big Rob had a storefront on the corner of Grey and Sycamore that sold food items. The store is usually run by him or his girl. Today it was him by himself. When he got the call that his hood got ripped to shreds he wasn't able to just leave and check on shit. He called his bitch and told her to hurry to the store because he had some urgent shit to check on.

Black & Frog had entered the store with their black gloves on. They both grabbed 2 Vitamin waters and headed to the counter. As planned I chirped Black saying, "yo, some crazy shit just happened in the Fruitbelt."

"Word? What happened?"

"I don't know but it's mad police and fire trucks out here."

"Damn, that's crazy. I wonder what happened."

"I don't know bruh. Where are you at anyway?"

"Me & Frog is at the store on Grey & Sycamore."

"Word? My man Big Rob owns that spot. In fact, he is from the Fruitbelt. Is he there?"

Big Rob heard the conversation as planned. He looked at Black when he heard his name over the chirp. Big Rob was curious who it was that knew him. Big Rob looked at Black and asked him, "who is that lil homie? I just heard my name through your chirp phone."

"Oh… You're Big Rob?"

"Yeah. Who was that you were talking to that knows me?"

Black said to me, "Bruh, Big Rob is here and he wants to know who you are."

"Well, introduce yourself after you tell him who I am."

"Alright bruh, I gotchu"

Black said to Big Rob, "This is my big homie from my block. I'm Black."

"What block are you from lil homie?"

"Box n Moe!!"

As soon as Black said our block shit changed. Big Rob knew then that Black was talking to me. He also knew in his heart that I was the reason the Fruitbelt was packed with them people. He also knew that he was only minutes away from his own demise. Big Rob tried to make a plea to Frog & Black, "please tell Chips that I apologize for the misunderstanding and I'll make it up to him."

Black left his phone pointed at Big Rob so that I can hear everything said. I sent Sleaze into the store. Upon seeing Sleaze Big Rob was truly scared. Sleaze said to Big Rob, "produce 100 bands in the next 5 minutes and Chips will let you live."

Without hesitation Big Rob said, "c'mon with me to the back." Big Rob led Sleaze & Frog into a back apartment and revealed a wall safe. Big Rob opened the safe and pulled out bundles and bundles of money out of it. Big Rob gave Frog a bag and started tossing bundles into it. "There are over 100 bands in here. Y'all can have it all. I don't want any problems."

"It's cool Big Rob. Chips is a man of his words. He's not gonna kill you."

The nigga show no courage and that shit really irritated me. He was acting like a straight bitch. "Thanks yo…. Tell Chips if I can help him with anything just let me know."

"Here, you tell him yourself. He's on the phone."

Big Rob got the phone and stammered, "he-he-hello?"

Within A Week

His scary ass only added to my confidence as I said, "Big Rob, sorry for this complicated situation that you find yourself in, but this is a bed that you've made yourself. Had you left well enough alone we both would've been getting bread and eating well. I don't like to take your paper but it's only fair. I do appreciate it though. I promise that I won't kill you. Just stay out of my way. Give my bruh the phone. Better yet, just put me on speaker." Big Rob did so and I said, "Frog, let him live for now."

"Are you serious?" Questioned Frog.

"Yeah. He can live until the next time I lay eyes on him," I said as I walked into the apartment. Frog looked at me, raised his pistol and squeezed the trigger at Big Robs face. The first shot lifted some of his forehead. The other 15 danced around his body like strippers on a nigga with bread. We walked out and jumped into the whips and bounced. What I didn't know at the time was that Big Rob's bitch had made it to the store and saw us leaving. What else I didn't know was that his bitch was a bitch that I knew from high school with. She identified me immediately.

CHAPTER 24

Damage & Shellz was driving down Genesee when Shellz said, "Cousin, ain't that the nigga Sleaze?"

"Where?"

"Right there at the stop light. The passenger in that oldsmobile."

"Hell yeah it is. Hold on, I'm about to bust a U."

Damage & Shellz was following us on our journey. They watched as we lit the Fruitbelt up. They followed us over to Big Rob's spot.

Shellz got to see what he was up against and said, "Kinfolk, them niggaz is CRAZY as FUCK!! Them niggaz got all kinds of guns with them. I've never seen nobody but Scarface with a fucking grenade launcher. Did you see how the nigga Sleaze was smiling as he let that shit blast?"

"Fuck them niggaz Shellz. You scared of them punks? They bleed just like us. At the right time I'm gonna roll up on that nigga Chips and pop 2 in his wig."

"Now is the time to get him. Wait, it's too late, he went into the store."

"Yeah, that was a good chance, but I'll be patient. I'll get him."

Damage had parked down the street for several minutes more. A bitch pulled up to the store and hopped out the car. It may have been 30 seconds but felt like minutes before Chips and his crew came up out of the store. After we pulled off, Damage & Shellz started to follow us again. When Damage got across from the store, the same girl came flying out of the store screaming!! Her screaming had thrown Damage off his game and he swerved into the other lane and scraped a car. It wasn't anything to call injury but it caused him to fall back. Being that he had lost me he went back to see what girly was screaming about. He pulled up on girly and asked, "hey, are you alright? Can I help you somehow?"

She was in hysterics as she said, "aww... They killed my boyfriend."

"Who? What are you talking about?"

"Chester!! Him and his friends killed my baby daddy."

"Are you sure? How do you know this?"

"The store is empty and my boyfriend is in the back apartment dead."

"Did you call the police yet?"

"Yes…. They said someone will be here shortly."

Damage rushed back to his car and got in and pulled off. He was deep in thought when Shellz asked, "what happened?"

"Them niggaz done killed the nigga in the store."

"Word?"

"On everything!! I wonder what the fuck is up with them dudes. This isn't like the Chips I know."

"Whatever is going on with him, he is dead ass serious. We'll have to be on full point when we run up on them niggaz. They're playing for keeps for real."

"I see….. I'm playing for keeps too cousin."

CHAPTER 25

"Good evening Ms. Jacobs. I'm Detective Denardo and this is my partner Detective Bickford. I'm sorry for your loss. I need to ask you some pertinent questions that'll help with the investigation. Are you feeling well enough to answer some questions?"

"Thank you. I'm fine enough to answer a few questions."

"What is your full name?"

"Chelsea Alyssa Jacobs."

"What's your relationship with the deceased?"

"The Deceased has a name!! It's Rob. Robert Griffith. He was my boyfriend!!"

"Sorry ma'am. How long have you known Mr. Griffith?"

"We've been together for 4 years."

"Can you tell me what happened today?"

"My boyfriend got murdered and you're asking stupid questions."

"Excuse me Ms. Jacobs," said Detective Bickford, "can you just tell us how your day began and lead us up to this point here? It'll really help us a lot."

She let out an exhausted breath and said, "I woke up and showered."

"Where'd you wake up?"

"In the apartment in the back of the store."

"Okay... Please continue."

"After I showered I got dressed and woke lil Rob up."

"Who's lil Rob?"

"He's our son. Mine and Rob's."

"I'm sorry. Please continue."

"When lil Rob was up and dressed I took him over to his grandmother's house in the Fruitbelt."

"The Fruitbelt? Where in the Fruitbelt?"

"On Rose street."

"Okay, what happened then?"

"After I dropped lil Rob off I came back here to open the store."

"What time would you say this was?"

"I open the store every day at 9 am."

"As you were opening the store what was your boyfriend Rob doing?"

"I don't know. When I came back from dropping our son off Rob was gone."

"Is that usual?"

"Yeah it is. He usually comes around noon to give me a bathroom run. Then we'll stay in the store together in the store until around 4 or 5 pm."

"So everything was usual until around that time?"

"Yes. At 5 pm I went to Roberts mother's house to pick up lil Rob. While sitting there I heard an awful sound and felt a small tremble. I thought we were having an earthquake. I ran to the window to look outside but didn't see anything out of place."

"What street does Rob's mother live on?"

"She lives on Grape street."

"Okay Ms. Jacobs, when you thought we were having an earthquake did you have any idea what was going on?"

"I had the slightest idea."

"Do you know what happened in the Fruitbelt today?"

"No. Not really. I wouldn't be surprised if there was some type of gang activity. Rob had called me shortly after that earthquake thing and said that it was urgent I get back to the store."

"Did he say what the urgency was?"

"No. He just told me to get my ass back here right now"

"What did you do then?"

"I gathered up lil Rob's things and came here."

"How long do you think it took you to get here?"

"Maybe 10 to 15 minutes."

"What did you do once you got here?"

"I went across the street to my sisters house to drop lil Rob off to her. When lil Rob was situated, I came over here."

"You came right in?"

"No. As I came out of my sister's house I saw 4 men leaving the apartment."

"These 4 men; can you tell us anything about them?"

"2 of the men looked like kids. The kids were wearing black gloves."

"Gloves?" Asked Detective Denardo.

"Yeah. Like baseball gloves."

"Did you see their faces? Did you recognize any of them?"

"Yes. There was one dude that I went to high school with."

"Really?" Detective asked anxiously. "Who was that? What is his name?"

"The guy I went to school with is Chester Chambers!!"

"How do you know it was Chester Chambers?"

"I told you that I went to school with him. He was the star basketball player and I was the head cheerleader. We were friends."

"Did you get to see the type of vehicle he was driving?"

"They drove off in 2 cars. I don't know a;; cars very well. I do know that both of the cars were dark in color."

Detective Bickford was ecstatic as he took notes. He was thinking that the men who killed Robert Griffith are the same men who turned the Fruitbelt into Iraq!!

Chelsea started crying again and she was unable to go any further with the interview. The Detectives wrapped things up and left Chelsea a card telling her to contact them if she can remember anything else.

While the interview was going on, the coroner came and picked up Rob's body. Live on the scene was channel 8 news reporting for the public. "Good evening Buffalo, this is Rachel Howard reporting live for channel 8 news. Earlier this evening on the east side of the city we had 2 horrific events take place. In the neighborhood known as the Fruitbelt; there were multiple murders. The person or persons responsible for this attack turned the neighborhood into a scene depicted from a horror movie. Nine people were killed and six are in critical condition due to a grenade being tossed. Immediately after the grenade tossing there was a series of rapid gun fire. People couldn't escape anywhere. We'll report more as we get it. This is Rachel Howard reporting for channel 8 news, Buffalo, New York."

CHAPTER 26

"Good evening Detectives Denardo and Bickford. I'm Special Agent Licass of the FBI head office here in Buffalo, N.Y."

"Good evening Agent Licass. How can we help you?" Asked Bickford.

"I hate to be the one to inform you but your local homicide department is no longer the lead investigators for the murders in the Fruitbelt or the Grey street killing."

"Sorry sir but I'm not following you here."

Agent Licass came closer to the 2 detectives and said, "the Buffalo homicide division is no longer in charge here. The Federal Government has taken the lead in this matter."

"How so? Why?"

"We've taken over because there was an explosive device used. That is along Federal guidelines and Federal crimes."

"So now we're off the case?" Asked Denardo.

"Absolutely not. I'll need you guys to assist me with your knowledge of the case. I'll also rather have you 2 guys with me being that you know more than anybody else."

"We're your guys," Denardo said.

"I think that you guys need to call home because there's no telling when you'll go there again," Licass stated.

* * * * *

"Okay gentlemen, let me give you a brief of who I am and why this case interests me." Agent Licass said.

"I thought you said that the Feds took the case over." Said Bickford.

"I am the Feds. We have the case. I took the case on personally"

"What's so personal about this case?"

"Are you guys familiar with TCB?"

"No. Not off hand. Why?"

"Well, TCB was a dangerous crew within a crew. The crew in itself was the Box n Moe Crew. A few from that organization formed a crew called TCB; which stands for The Caddy Boyz."

"I've heard of them. They were some weed dealers right?"

"Right and wrong. They did sell weed and they were major dealers. They were thugs and killers first. They killed a snitch of mine and they killed 2 narcotic officers kids. They've also killed a few known and unknown street thugs. We had no type of evidence to bring them to court. The few witnesses we had ended up dead. They've been relatively low-key until now."

"Which Box n Moe members were a part of this TCB crew?"

"There were 5 very close members. One is in prison forever. His name is Erik or Eazy as they called him. Another member is Low; who's been missing or just haven't been seen or heard from. Then there was their main killer Zack!! Zack was shot down and murdered himself. The other 2 members are still around and running shit; Gator & Dawg!! Gator is the intelligence within their setup. He ran them very well. They've made a lot of money and got away with a lot of killings. Dawg is a ruthless and reckless killer. We believe that Dawg is the trigger man behind the 2 officers' sons. Before the sons got killed we Dawg on a great case that consisted of conspiracy to distribute, possess and extortion. Then our witness get killed trying to put the final dagger into Dawg. The rest is history. I want them pieces of shit bad. I want involvement with all things Box n Moe."

"Are you familiar with Chester Chambers?" Asked Denardo.

"Chester Chambers? Does he have a street name?"

"If he does we don't know what it is yet. The Chester Chambers in our files is an older gentleman who's a drug addict known for committing petty crimes to feed his habit. The Chester Chambers we have is in ECMC on life support. He has been there for several days now. We know that it couldn't be him."

"Does he have children?"

"We're waiting for that report to come in. Can the FBI help get the information sooner?" Asked Bickford.

"I'll call the office and get someone on it. Does the person who identified this Chester Chambers have any photos?" Asked Agent Licass.

"You know what? Chelsea Jacobs said that Chester Chambers was the star basketball player in high school. I'll contact Ms. Jacobs and find out what school it was that they attended together."

Detective Denardo called Ms. Jacobs and Ms. Jacobs mother answered the phone on the third ring, "hello."

"Good evening. This is Detective Denardo of the Buffalo Homicide Division. I'm sorry to bother you but I need to speak with Ms. Chelsea Jacobs please?"

"Hi detective. Unfortunately my daughter took a sedative and she's out like a light. Is there anything I can help you with?"

"Perhaps you can. What high school did your daughter attend?"

"She went to SouthPark high school."

"Do you know if she has any year books?"

"Certainly. She has the yearbooks for her last three years."

"Is it possible for me to come pick them up? I'll return them I promise."

"May I ask why?"

"Well, we're trying to identify a suspect and Chelsea said that he went to school with her."

"Oh…. Well sure. Come get them. They're sitting right here. I guess that Chelsea figured you'd come asking for them. Do you know where I live?"

"Unfortunately not. Can you give me the address please? By the way, I never got your name."

Within A Week

"My name is Krystal Jacobs. I live at 95 Peach street."

"The front or back door?"

"The front will be fine. I'll see you when you get here Detective."

"Alright Ms. Jacobs, I'll see you shortly."

Detective Denardo turned to his partner Bickford and Agent Licass and said, "Ms. Jacob's mother said that I can come get the yearbooks of her daughters high school years. Ms. Jacobs said that Chester Chambers was the star basketball player. I'm sure that those books will have a photo of Mr. Chambers."

Agent Licass said, "very good work detective. Shall we be on our way?"

The three lawmen got into a car and headed back to the Fruitbelt once again.

* * * * *

After retrieving the yearbooks, the lawmen examined each one with an Eagle's eye. They found a picture of me from my senior year and immediately phoned that bitch from channel 8 news. They had faxed Rachel Howard of channel 8 news the picture of me and she immediately went on set and live. "This is Rachel Howard with channel 8 news. We have breaking news concerning a lot of the violent activity that erupted today in our city. The Buffalo police were diligently combing the streets and other sources and they've come up with a suspect for the brutal slaying of a store owner on Grey street. In the left hand corner of your screen is the man being sought for the murder of Robert Griffith. The man depicted in the photo is 28 year old Chester Chambers. He is considered armed and extremely dangerous. If you see this man please don't attempt to do anything but stay away and contact the police as fast as you can at 847-0010 or just 911. We'll have round the clock coverage until the streets are deemed safer. Reporting live from channel 8 news; I'm Rachel Howard."

CHAPTER 27

After that fucking broadcast ended my phone started ringing off the hook. I ignored a few of those calls because they were by people whose just being nosey and don't really fuck with me. However, I did answer Dawg's call, "what up Dawg?"

"Damn S

un, I just caught the news and shit is serious huh man?"

"Hell yeah!! I wonder how the devils got my picture. I wonder how they even know it was me."

"Did you get the video tape from the store?"

"Hell yeah!! Black snatched it up when we had Rob in the back."

"Black's pretty thorough."

"Fuck it Dawg, it is what it's gon be."

"You already know that we got yo back through thick and thin. Whatever you need or want just hit me up."

"Yeah I know you boyz are there for me but don't sweat it. Y'all boyz do y'all. I'll be cool."

"Alright Sun, hit me up if you need me"

"Bet"

After getting off the horn with Dawg I just sat back and contemplated my next move. Shit was already fucked so I might as well go all out with a bang right? With that thought in mind I went to sleep to get rested.

* * * * *

Within A Week

There was a loud bang on my door that woke me with a start. I immediately grabbed my burner ready for death action. Just so you know, I have a gun handy every 10 steps I take. Anyway, nothing burst into my spot so I went to the door with a gun ready to blast. Behind me I can hear Sleazes ringtone. I peeked through the peephole to see Sleaze, Black and Frog standing there. I opened the door and they poured inside. Sleaze hugged me tightly and said, "You're not alone my nigga. We're here with you until the end of time."

"Thanks my nigga but this is where we part. Them devils don't know nothing about y'all niggaz. Y'all got a free pass to enjoy life. Just remember me and rep me to the fullest."

"Fuck that bullshit you talking about bruh. We're ready to go find everybody that's looking for you. Especially Damage."

"Man, fuck Damage. He's the last on my mind."

"I feel like you do. We're ready to get at Buffalo's finest!!"

"Huh?" I asked perplexed.

"Yeah my nig; I'm talking about going up to the police station and taking some of them bitches with us. We'll make gangsta history!! Most mass killings involve schools or kids or defenseless people. We can go bang with the best," said Black with a straight face.

I looked at the 3 goons in front of me and said, "Y'all niggaz not ready for something like that."

"I bet we are. C'mon, let's roll my nigga."

"Fuck it then. Let's roll a few dutches and get our guns ready and strap up our vests. After we're right we can go right on Fillmore & Ferry and tear that bitch up!!"

* * * * *

Once again we drove in two seperate cars. Sleaze was mad determined that we ride together. We followed each other and then split up on our approach. The 2 young niggaz approached from the Ferry way and we came up Woodlawn. Both cars pulled into the police stations parking lot at the same time. A patrol car rode pass us on it's way to fuck with niggaz in the streets. Once the patrol car was gone we exited our whips fully strapped. I had a tapped together double clipped K-Cutter with extra clips. I also had twin .44 mags with hollow shells in extended clips. The ammo that wasn't hollow tipped was armor piercing. Of course Sleaze had the grenade launcher M-16. He had several clips and a pair of .45 auto's. Black carried 2 Macs and he also had a sawed off 16 gauge. Frog carried a street sweeper with 100 round clips taped together. I asked him why he chose the street sweeper and he said, "I don't have to aim. Just let this shit roar like the Lion it is."

Sleaze aimed the launcher at the backdoor and pulled the trigger. The door & most of its surroundings blew inward. We poured in with me leading the way. I took a right with Sleaze right on my heels. The 2 young gunners went left. The huge explosion from the grenade caused several officers to leave their offices to investigate with guns drawn. The first cop that was in my sights was a bitch! I released the K and the shells ripped across her face. The next 2 cops that presented a target were torn down by Sleazes M-16. One cop got hit in the neck. He spun and collapsed against a wall. The cop next to him got lucky and died from a headshot with his brain matter spread on the wall behind him. Out of nowhere another cop appeared. This fucker had got off 3 rapid shots. All 3 shots hit me squarely in the chest. It didn't bother me none because I had on a vest just like the street cops wore. The bullets literally bounced off. I squeezed the K at his ass with anger and let a gang of rounds get him. He wasn't wearing a vest so the damage my shells caused was really ugly.

Behind us I was able to hear rapid fire from Black's Macs going off and the typewriter sound of the street sweeper that Frog was clapping. Every few seconds I heard screams and cries of the police that were being abused by those shells. Ahead of us was a door labelled conference room C. The door was closed but we could the hiss of walkie talkies being used. I stepped back and allowed Sleaze room to open the door with a grenade round. Again he smiled with happiness to use the grenade once more. He pointed, squeezed and blew the door and some wall down. No sooner then the door fell I was filling the space busting my K. I pulled a Frog and didn't aim at shit. I just filled every corner of the room with multiple rounds. It must have been some type of conference there or something because there were maybe a dozen cops in there. The grenade had killed or mangled about 7 of them and my cutter knocked off the rest.

Some patrol cars must've been summoned. We heard tires screeching out back the way we came in. Not long after I heard Black yell that Frog was down. When we heard that we turned around and rushed in that direction. Through spurts of gunfire we heard Black yelling, "you dirty fucking pigs!! I'm gonna kill all you rotten muthafuckaz!!"

The cops that snuck up on Frog didn't hear or see us as we approached from behind them. We pulled out our pistols and took aim from about 20 feet and emptied the clip. Two cops collapsed without a word because our rounds entered their heads from the back and exited through their mouths. The other 2 cops that were with them saw them fall and turned around just in time to catch some bullets in the mouth and throats. They gurgled whatever words they wanted to say.

Black ran up to us and said, "these the devils that shot Frog. In fact, it was this redneck muthafucka right here." He then walked over to the dead cop and emptied a clip into the cops face and spit on the dead man. Sleaze & I walked over to where Frogs limp body lay crumpled on the tile floor. Frog got hit on the side of his head and the exit wound was his lower jaw. My stomach churned at the sight of my lil man sprawled out on the floor dead. Sleaze begins to cry. Between his sobs he was saying, "I swear on my momma Frog, I'm gonna make every cop pay for this shit." After standing up and crossing my heart to bless Frogs soul I heard a loud bang!! I fell to the floor and watched as the blood from my neck wound poured all over the floor around me. My subconscious mind was hearing Sleaze saying, "Chips!! Chips!!" That's when I woke up from that horrible dream dripping and pouring with sweat!!

CHAPTER 28

"Yo Chips!! Answer the door nigga!!" Yelled Sleaze.

I wiped the sweat from my brow and yelled back, "Here I come nigga. Relax yo ass some. You knock like you the po-po.

I opened the door and he said, "what the fuck? You look like shit my nigga!!"

"I feel like shit too. I just had the most fucked up dream."

"Yeah? What was it about?"

"We ran up in the police station and bodied everything!!"

"Not a bad dream at all."

"Frog got killed in the process."

"Yeah... That's a fucked up dream."

"You don't have to tell me. What the fuck was you bangin on my door like you are the police. What's going on?"

"Shit; I called almost 30 times but didn't get no answer. I'm sure that you've seen yourself on TV. I was just checking up on you."

"Me being on TV wasn't part of the dream?"

"What?"

"I mean the news flashing my picture for the whole town to see."

"You don't remember talking to Dawg? That shit is real my nigga. The law is looking for you." Sleaze stated.

"Oh well, it really doesn't matter anyway. I'm dying this week so they'll only get a few days out of me if I don't die first."

"Wrong attitude my dude."

"Yeah yeah yeah" I said sarcastically.

Within A Week

"Listen Chips, let's get outta town before someone rat you out and the boyz come kicking in yo doors."

"Out of town like running?"

"Nah. Let's just get out for the night or two. I booked 3 rooms at the Holiday Inn out by the airport. I figured that we could lay-low there for a while until you come up with the next move."

"I've figured our next move already."

"Oh yeah? What is it?" Sleaze asked.

"We're gonna set shit up to pop Damage top."

"I'm with that. What's the set up?"

"C'mon, let's get out of here and I'll explain it in the car."

Inside the car I told Sleaze that he's gonna call them 2 badass white bitches from the strip club. I told him to set it up for them to come out to a different hotel up the street. "Tell them that they're gonna hit you and ya man off with some of that pussy. Make them think you're giving each of them a stack for that ass. They're gonna tell Damage of the plan and he'll try to set something up for you or us. Me & Frog will be in a room across from yours peeping through the peephole waiting for Damage. When he shows up I'll blast his ass from the back."

"What makes you think that Damage will show?"

"Them white bitches are his bitches. If not his, they're his bitches bitches. Not only that, he wants to kill me!! I got so deep under his skin for walking him for them 10 bricks. I got further under it when I spoke to him like he wasn't about that!! I got even deeper when we got his ass for those diamonds. He's gonna show my dude!!"

"Alright bruh that's what's up. When should I call them hoes?"

"Wait until we get everything set up. Call Black & Frog and tell them to come out to the telly pronto."

CHAPTER 29

"Peaches, you won't believe who just called me," said Cream.

"Bitch, who called you?"

"That dude from the other night."

"There's a lot of dudes from the other night."

"Yeah you right. I'm talking about the one that got a private dance from both of us!!"

"Bitch be more specific. A lot of dudes got the treatment from both of us!!"

"Girl I'm talking about the dude that Damage wants so bad."

"That Sleaze dude?"

"Yeah... Him."

"What did he say? What did he want?"

"He said that he wanted to hook up," Cream said.

"When did he call?"

"About 10 minutes ago."

"What did you tell him? Hold up, my phone is ringing."

Peaches looked at her phone display and noticed the number wasn't familiar to her. She hesitantly answered, "Hello... Who is this?"

Sleaze said, "damn sexy, is that how you answer a call?"

"I do when I don't recognize the caller. Who is this?"

"This ya boy Sleaze. Remember me?"

"Of course I remember you. What took you so long to call me? What's up?"

Within A Week

"Damn, don't sound so excited to hear from me!!"

"Anyway….. What's good? My private dance wasn't good enough for you?"

"Your dance was really good. I've just been busy lately."

"Your free now?"

"Yeah… Only for tonight though."

"Just for tonight huh? So what's up?"

"I'm trying to see you is what's up."

"Sorry baby, I gotta work tonight."

"Yo fine ass can make more paper with me and my homie than the club tonight!!"

"Really? Is that so?"

"Hell yeah that's so!!"

"How much paper are you talking about?"

"We got a stack each."

"You and yo man? Would you like me to bring my sister?"

"Hell yeah…. I had called her before I called you."

"She was just trying to tell me something like that before you called."

"Yeah, so what's up?"

"We can make it happen. When and where?"

"I'm about to get a hotel. I'll call you later with the info."

"Alright… I'll be waiting to hear from you."

Peaches turned to Cream and shared with her the conversation she just had. Cream said, "Call Kandy so she can tell Damage what's going on. Damage has been stressing over these niggaz. He'll appreciate us for this."

* * * * *

"Kandy!! Kandy!!" yelled Peaches

Kandy came strolling into the dining room where Peaches & Cream was sitting and talking. Kandy said, "which one of you bitches calling my name like she's crazy?"

"That would be this bitch," Cream said as she pointed to her sister.

"Well I'm here. What is it?"

"Me & Cream just got a call from that Sleaze dude!!"

"Bitch stop playing"

"I'm not playing, am I Cream?"

"Nope. He called trying to get some pussy," Cream stated.

"He called you too bitch?"

"Hell yeah. He said that he has a homeboy."

Kandy didn't pause when she said, "Alright, hook that shit up. I'm about to call Damage."

When Damage & Shellz got back to Kandy's condo, Damage told the girls to meet them in the living room. When all was present, Damage clicked on the flat screen TV and turned it to channel 8. As he expected, the newscaster Rachel Howard was reporting and showing Chip's picture. Everybody sat quietly as the news was being told. Rachel was basically repeating the same earlier news. All watched with keen interest. When the segment was over Damage said, "I wonder what got into that nigga? He was never violent like this. Kandy, what was so important for me to rush here?"

"The dude Sleaze called Peaches & Cream."

"Word? What did he want?"

In unison the twins said, "some pussy."

"What did y'all say? Did y'all hook it up?"

"We told him that we'll be available later."

"Good. Make sure that y'all give me all the details as soon as y'all get it."

"We got you," the twins said together again.

* * * * *

"Cash, I need a favor from you."

"Damage you know that my favors cost paper."

"I already know and I got you."

"Cool, what's up my G?"

"I have a situation that cause for 2 gunners."

"Talk baby, you're not saying anything."

"What's the number on that?"

"How many niggaz you want dead?"

"Just two."

"That will be 8 stacks."

"Cool. I'll meet you in our spot in an hour."

"Have that bread with you."

"Don't I always?" Asked Damage before ending the call.

Damage turned to Shellz and said, "The shit that's going on with Chips is really strange. Since he had that accident his whole persona changed. His boy Sleaze calling them hoes is kinda weird too!!"

"Why do you say that?"

"Chips gotta know that Peaches & Cream is part of my shit. Why would he allow his man Sleaze to hit the hoes up if that nigga ain't trying to set me up?"

"Maybe the nigga Sleaze is thinking with his dick and making this move behind Chips back."

"That's possible but I highly doubt it."

"So who is this Cash dude? What is he about?"

"Cash is a freelance killer. I pay him to put in work for me from time to time," Damage said.

"What's he gonna do with our situation?"

"I'm using him just in case Chips is trying to set me up. I'm gonna swallow my pride and let Cash knock his block off his shoulders."

"That's smart."

"Sometimes you gotta strategize instead of always being reckless."

"That's for sho," Shellz said as he let his accent hang.

Damage phone rang and he said to Shellz, "this them hoes." He answered and just listened for a minute before he replied with, "alright Peaches, text it to me and make sure that you keep your phone handy."

Damage was smiling while driving to see Cash. Shellz looked over and asked, "what are you smiling about? What was said?"

"Peaches said that the nigga Sleaze called and told them to meet him at a bar out by the airport. She also gave me a website where I can track her phone. I'm gonna let them hoes get Sleaze comfortable and have Cash move on him."

"Okay. What's our play?"

"Smoke some of this bomb shit and chill until I get the call from Cash."

CHAPTER 30

At Slick's Tavern out by the airport, Black sat in the parking lot waiting for Peaches & Cream. Before he left for the Bar he asked Sleaze, "how will I know it's them?"

"Because these 2 white bitches are fine as fuck. Their bodies are like Coco's and their faces are pretty as ever. You'll know bruh. If you see 2 fine ass twinz just say, "Peaches & Cream."

Black was waiting for about 45 minutes when a Range Rover came into the parking lot and dropped 2 of the coldest white bitches that Black has ever seen. Before the girls were able to venture into the bar Black called their names, "Peaches & Cream."

They both turned at the sound of their names being called and scanned the parked cars. Black saw them searching so he flicked his lights a few times to grab their attention. The twinz cautiously walked over to the car and peered in. None of the women recognized Black so Peaches asked, "do we know you?"

"Not right now you don't, but y'all we shortly."

"Is that right? Who are you and how do you know our names?"

"My brother Sleaze told me y'all name. I'm Black."

"Where is your brother?" Asked Cream.

"He's nearby. He wanted me to pick y'all up."

"We're not getting in a car with a stranger. Can you call your brother?"

"Yeah baby girl, hold up a second," said Black as he dialed Sleaze number..

Sleaze answered. "What up bruh?"

"I got the girls here but they said they are not getting in a car with a stranger."

"Alright, sit tight, I'm about to call them."

"Cool. I'll tell them."

The girls heard Blacks side of the conversation and asked, "tell us what?"

"He said that he's about to call y'all."

No sooner than Black saying that Creams phone rang. "Hello."

"What up Beautiful? Y'all not trying to roll with my brother?" Asked Sleaze.

"We don't know him and that wasn't part of the plan."

"The plan was for y'all to get dropped off and picked up!!"

"Yeah.. Dropped off by our people and picked up by you!!"

"Listen sweetheart, I just wanna chill with y'all. My intentions are honest and my brother is rolling with me. Y'all can ride with him to where I'm at or y'all can get a cab back to where y'all gonna go. He'll give you the bread for a cab or you can come get this bread I got for you. So tell me something."

"Listen dude, We need another $500 on top for both of us. You better fuck good too!!" Cream stated.

"I got y'all. I'm gonna break that pussy off something proper."

Peaches & Cream got in the car with Black. Sleaze had a room adjoining with another and a room directly across from the room they'll be in. The room next door to them will be empty just in case Sleaze & Black need an escape route. Me & Frog was in the room across from they're room. As Black led the twinz into the room, Frog was at the door watching and said, "Damn!! Them Monkeys are fine as fuck!! Them niggaz are about to have a blast until they have to blast."

Behind Frog I said, "yeah, them some cold joints."

"Will I be able to hit later?"

"If shit goes well and we don't have to body nobody we'll both smash."

Within A Week

"Alright bet."

"Until then lil homie keep your eyes on the prize."

* * * * *

Damage & Shellz lead the way for Cash and his homie Ice. Damage was following Peaches phone signal. They tracked the phone's signal to the Econo Lodge hotel located on the corners of Cleveland Hill Rd and Transit Rd. The hotel wasn't a 5 star establishment but was decent. Their rooms were concealed from the main street. On Transit Rd across from the hotel there was a plaza that held a Marshalls and a T.J Maxx department store; along with many other establishments.

Damage & Shellz had parked in the plaza's parking lot to watch the hotel from there while Cash & Ice went into the hotel to get a feel of the layout.

Peaches & Cream was inside room 112 on the first floor with Sleaze & Black. Sleaze was on one bed with Cream while Black was on the other with Peaches. Both women were laying a wild and crazy display of sucking dick. Peaches took the less experienced Black to the back of her throat and forced him to bust off in her mouth. She swallowed him back and got up to fetch something to drink; only to find the ice bucket empty of beverages and ice. Peaches had hoped that would be the case because it gave her the opportunity to leave the room and go down to the ice machine and get more ice and drinks. At the same time she could leave the rooms key card for Cash & Ice.

After casing the hotel, Cash & Ice made their way to the spot where one of the twinz was supposed to leave a card key. Entering the refreshment room, Cash literally bumped into Peaches. They looked into each others eyes and knew that they were on the same team. Cash reached down and squeezed Peaches phat ass and said, "after this business is done I gotta hit this!!"

She responded with, "you'll have enough paper to hit it when it's over." Then she smirked and walked off.

When Peaches left the room Black got off the bed he was on and got on the bed with Sleaze and Cream. She was giving Sleaze some major head while shaking her phat ass in Blacks direction. Seeing Cream's juicy ass in the air swinging back and forth had got the young boy instantly hard again. Black got behind Cream and slid deep inside her wet pussy. She gasped when he entered her but didn't lose a beat with her head performance. In fact, she began to suck more fiercely. Young Black was smashing her spot and her body began to tremble and shake as she let out a howl that told him that she was cumming. Before Sleaze or Black was able to get off the door opened and Peaches walked back in. She looked at the scene on the bed and her face scrunched up into anger. She said to her sister, "get up slut, we need to talk. In the bathroom. Now!!" When the girls made their way to the bathroom, Sleraze & Black stood up and grabbed their clothes. They grabbed their burners from they're spots and opened the door to the connecting room for Frog to come in.

When Peaches left the room for the ice, Frog had left me in the room as he went to room 113. We had our chirps on low & buzz. I chirped Sleaze phone as our signal that shit was about to get ugly real soon. Sleaze buzzed me back when Frog got there. I put my face to the peep hole and paid mad attention to their room door.

The twinz came out of the bathroom to find Sleaze, Black and Frog standing with guns in hand watching them and the door. The twinz felt it in their hearts that shit wasn't gonna go as planned and they were trapped in the middle of everything. Peaches tried to be smart and flip the scene by saying, "what the fuck is this? First y'all run a train on my sister and now y'all got some other dude here with guns in hand, is this a robbery Sleaze? This how you get down? We're outta here dude."

"'Bitch please!! Neither of you bitches is calling anybody and y'all not going anywhere. Your sister wanted a train ran on her and we've been on to y'all. You bitches are part of Damage crew."

"What the hell are you talking about?" Asked Peaches.

Sleaze had pushed the couch in front of the door and said, "sit yo monkey ass down bitch," as he pointed with his gun to the couch.

Within A Week

The girls sat down reluctantly. Frog & Black stood to the side of them in an angle that gave them clear paths for their bullets to fly. Sleaze said, "if nobody tries to come in here in the next 10 minutes than we can get back to having fun and y'all can leave here afterwards with about 3 stacks each. If someone does try to come in then y'all better try not to get hit!! Actually, it doesn't matter what y'all do because if someone does try to come in, y'all hoes dying first!!"

CHAPTER 31

About 6 minutes went by without a peep from anybody. I was still watching room 112 from my peephole across the hall. Everything was quiet and I was a bit jumpy. I was startled when my phone chirped with Black's voice following through the speaker, "is everything gravy OG?"

"So far. Tell Frog I said to go back into room 113 and wait at the door leading to the hall.

Black relayed my demands and reported that Frog is in position. No sooner than I heard that I saw a hooded nigga past the room that Frog was in. I alerted Sleaze and he turned BET on high volume. The same hooded nigga came by again and this time he stopped in front of room 112, reached inside his hood pocket and produced a keycard.

Frog was looking through his peephole and saw the same hooded nigga walk past. Frog was itching to bust his gun. When the hooded nigga inserted the keycard and tried to push the door open he wasn't expecting to find resistance. He got a small look between the cracks and saw that the twinz was seated on a couch blocking the entrance of the room. Ice pushed hard on the door to give himself room to enter. Ice entered with his burner in front of him looking for a target. Seconds later Frog burst from room 113 and I burst from the room directly across and behind the nigga. Frog was so anxious to pop a top that he didn't look behind himself as he came outta the room cause if he did he would've seen another hooded nigga round the corner

Within A Week

behind him. While Frog was trying to creep, Cash was raising his beretta. It only took 1 shot to push Frog's wig against the wall. Frog died instantly. There was no shaking or trembling. The explosion from Cash's gun ignited a barrage of gunfire. Sleaze & Black jumped from behind the wall at the same time that Ice was turning into the hall. That was a major mistake on Ice's behalf because Sleaze & Black had their hammers at the ready and opened fired at the sight of him. Ice had turned the wrong way when he turned the corner and he had his back to the dual. Their bullets ran up his back until they found the back of his head and pushed through his skull. Twenty rounds were let off and all but 8 hit Ice. The 8 that didn't hit Ice had found its way to the Twinz bodys. Peaches was thrown to the floor from the impact of the rounds that hit her in the head and face. Sad to say that she died slowly. Good for that bitch!! Cream got hit in the high neck area and shoulder. She was stretched out on the couch but still breathing. She was conscious but unable to move because of paralysis.

Cash had killed a lot of people and that gave him the notion that he was the killer and can't be killed because came storming through like he was invincible.

Let me explain something to you before I carry on what happened next. Remember that dream I had concerning Frog getting killed in the police station? Well, when I saw Frog slumped against the wall, I froze up!! I mean I really froze up. Not a nerve twitched. I was stunned beyond belief. I heard all the gunfire going on across the hall but I was still standing motionless looking at Frog's dead body. I heard a bitch scream. A nigga yell and hit the floor. Still no reaction by me. I just stood behind the door with one hand on the knob and the other clutching my calico. When the gunfire ceased I came out of my trance and heard footsteps in the hall. My trance gave me the advantage and the drop on the other hooded nigga. He came through looking in one direction. When he got to the door of 112 I swung open my door and was back into my murder mind. The nigga heard the door and turned in my direction and knew that he was had. The look we shared with each other was like a baby gazelle and a lion. My calico was already adjusted on his face. He blinked and that caused my finger to react. A burst of 3 rounds exploded out of my burner and entered his face. His dead body hit the ground and I calmly walked over to him and dumped the rest of my mag into his body. He was left mangled and tattered.

Sleaze & Black crept through the room of 113 and came into the hallway. They saw frog's dead body sprawled on the floor and then they saw me standing over a dead body with my gun clicking because there were no more shells in it. Black brought me out of my trance, "Chips!! Chips!! C'mon homie, we gotta get outta here."

"Yeah, c'mon bruh. We gotta breeze," Sleaze said behind Black.

I looked at them and slowly walked in their direction. I had big tears streaming down my face. I was so fucked up behind Frog's killing. He was so young and official. Here it is he's dead behind my bullshit!! We emptied Frog's pockets of the car keys and weapons. We didn't want Frog to look like a participant. We bounded out the side door and jumped into our whips. I was still kinda fucked up mentally so Black had to drive alone while Sleaze drove me back to the hotel we had rented.

CHAPTER 32

Damage & Shellz saw the 2 cars speeding from behind the hotel. He was expecting to hear from one of the twinz or even Cash. He called Peaches and Creams phone to no avail. He called Cash's phone and didn't get an answer there either. Damage said to Shellz, "I wonder what happened. Wanna run over there and see what happened?"

"Yeah, we can do that."

They drove over to the hotel and parked out back. They entered the hotel through the side door that we exited from. Damage & Shellz immediately smelled the gun smoke throughout the hall. They rounded a corner and saw 2 dead men on the floor in close proximity. Damage recognized Cash by the clothes he was wearing upon entering the hotel. Shellz said, "Damn kinfolk, it looks like them boyz was ready for a attack."

"Yeah. Who is that muthafucka over there?"

"C'mon cuz, let's check the room and see if the girls are alright."

"Yeah. Let's do that."

Damage led the way into the room of 112 and stopped short. He saw a pair of sneakers just around a wall and knew that Cash's boy Ice was dead also. Damage took a step and felt something crunch under his foot. That caused him to look down and when he did he saw Peaches on the floor with half her head missing. He looked on the couch and saw Cream laying there in a puddle of blood. He looked into her face and was able to see that she was still alive. He cupped her head to his chest and told her to just hold on because help will be there soon. Several seconds later the police piled into the room with guns drawn ready to kill some niggaz. Seeing that there was no resistance from Damage & Shellz, the police had searched and cuffed them; then rushed them to headquarters for an intensive interview.

* * * * *

After being escorted to the Homicide Headquarters in downtown Buffalo, Damage was led upstairs to interview room C. Waiting inside the room was detectives Denardo & Bickford. Also present was a Agent Licass of the FBI. Upon entering the room Damage noticed cookies and snacks sitting on the table. Detective Denardo offered Damage a seat and some snacks; which Damage declined the snacks and took a seat. "I'm homicide detective Denardo. Mr. Lewis what were you doing in that hotel room?"

"I've already told you dudes."

"No you haven't. You may have told someone else but you hadn't told me."

"I went there to check on some friends for my girlfriend."

"Who are your girl's friends?"

"Denise & Danielle. The 2 women."

"How do you know them?"

"I just told you that they're my girl's friends. They work with my girl at a strip club."

"Why were you there if those women are your girlfriend friends?"

Damage looked at the other detectives and asked, "what's wrong with this dude? He didn't hear me the first time?"

The FBI agent said, "just answer the fucking question dickhead!!"

"I went to check on them for my girlfriend."

Agent Licass asked, "was your girlfriend at the hotel too? Why would you have to go check on them?"

"Nah she wasn't there. My girl dropped them off to see someone who wanted to party with the twinz."

"Why would your girl send you to check on them?"

Because the girls didn't show up for work and weren't answering their phones. So my girl called me and asked me to go check on them."

"What's your girlfriend's name?"

"Kandace Leonard."

"We'll be needing to speak with her sooner than later."

"Do what you need."

"Do you know anyone else that was at that hotel Mr. Lewis?" Asked Bickford.

"Nah, I don't."

"Are you sure?"

"What's with these stupid as questions? I just said that I don't know anyone else but the twinz."

Agent Licass ended the interview with, "We're gonna run a gunshot test on you. We're also gonna keep and test your clothing. We're also gonna examine your phone."

Damage didn't care about any of that because he left his phone that contained Cash number, his guns and anything else that can harm him in his car. Kandy had someone pick his car up and park it somewhere else. Damage said, "whatever man. Do whatever you feel is necessary."

"Thanks for your cooperation. Please follow detective Bickford and after he's done you can go. Don't leave town because we may need to speak with you again."

"Yeah…. Alright."

CHAPTER 33

The following morning I was awakened to the TV showing the fuck shit that happened at the hotel up the street. As usual, it was that bitch Rachel Howard reporting. "Good morning, this is Rachel Howard with the channel 8 news. Sometime during the early morning hours more violence has found its way into our area. In this hotel behind me the police responded to a call of shots fired and was greeted with dead bodies. They discovered 4 people dead; all riddled with bullets. One of the victims was shot beyond recognition. Throughout the violence there was 1 survivor who was left for dead. That person was able to give the authorities the name of 2 men that were responsible for the shootings. One of the people of interest is already being sought by the Buffalo police for another killing. The other person of interest goes by the name of "Sleaze". The police have yet to put a face with the name but they're diligently working on it. The police believe that Sleaze is the partner of Chester Chambers. Mr. Chambers is wanted in connection with the slaughter that happened in the Fruitbelt and the killing of Robert Griffith yesterday. If you happen to see Chester Chambers, please don't try to subdue him yourself. Immediately contact the Buffalo police. None of the 4 victims names have been released until the family have been notified. The lone survivor is in ECMC with severe spinal injuries and is listed in critical condition. This is Rachel Howard reporting live for channel 8 news."

Within A Week

That dumb bitch made sure that she plastered my picture up for several minutes for the city to see me clearly. I should just go all out and go by there and slump her ass just for the fuck of it.

Sleaze & Black was still asleep when that segment came on. I couldn't sleep because I was depressed behind Frog's death. I called gator and he informed me that they caught the news and was wondering who the 4 people dead are. I told him how I was trying to set Damage up and he tried to set me up at the same time. Instead of his bitch-ass showing up he sent some shooters of his own. When I told Gator that we killed the 2 shooters and 1 of the stripper bitches he was cool. When I told him that also killed was our lil nigga Frog, he got real quiet. After a moment of silence I told him that the police have no idea about Black. I told him that Black is a real thoroughbred and I need for him to call Black back to the hood just to keep him safe. The jakes are after me & Sleaze and there wasn't any reason to continue on with a ending that he can avoid. Gator agreed to what I was saying and said that he'll get Black under his wings.

As I was sitting there reloading our guns, I heard Black's personal phone ringing. Black was laid out and didn't hear shit so I answered it for him because I knew it was Gator. I woke Black up and gave him the phone. He said in a groggy voice, "hello?" I was only able to hear Blacks side of the conversation. What I heard him say was, "say word!!" Then he said, "alright, I'll be through later." Then he said, "right now?" Then, "alright, let me holla at Chips. I'll call you when I'm on my way." Then he hung up.

Black looked at me and said, "Gator needs me right quick. I'm gonna run to the hood real quick if it's cool with you."

"It's cool. We're just gonna lay low until I think of a plan. Go handle whatever you need to for Gator. Call me later."

"Should I tell Gator to come scoop me or will one of y'all drop me off?"

"Take yourself. Hold the olds down. We're better off with one whip right now anyway."

"Cool. You need anything while I'm in the hood?"

"Nah lil nigga, I'm good. Stay safe and I'll see you when we meet up again." I gave him a hug and hid my tears because I won't see him again.

After Black had left I woke Sleaze up and turned the TV back on. We smoked some good and watched the news together. When the news was finally over Sleaze then realized that Black was gone. He asked, "Where is Black?"

"I had Gator call for him."

"Why? He's thorough and really about that life!!"

"That's exactly why I had Gator call for him. Black is a good and smart kid. He'll run the streets one day. This isn't his time to die or get locked up forever. We lost Frog already. His lost was too much. The cops don't know anything about Black and I don't intend for them to find him with us once we face them faggots in the streets. It doesn't make sense to have him trapped off when he doesn't have to be."

"Yeah.. You're right."

"Sleaze, you do know that once we get back in the streets I'll be recognized. The person or people that see me will call the cops!!"

"Yeah I know that. You're saying that to say what?"

"I'm just telling you to be on point. We may have to bust our guns right away."

"Bruh, you already know that I'm down for that gun clappin action."

"Alright cool. Let me jump in the shower."

When I got out of the shower I decided to call Nurse Nakesha. She answered right away, "oh my god Chester. Are you alright? I've seen the news and I know that a mistake is being made."

"I'm good Beautiful. How are you? Did you look into that situation I asked you about?"

"Yeah I did. Something weird is going though. In our computers there's only 1 Chester Chambers admitted and it says that he had some sort of auto accident and he's been diagnosed with a fatal form of Cancer. It also says that he left the hospital without being released by the doctor."

Within A Week

"Damn…. This shit doesn't make any sense at all."

"Is there anything else I can do for you baby?"

"Do you have to work today?"

"I'm at work right now."

"On your break can you check the Cancer floor and see if there's another Chester Chambers there?"

"When will you call back?" She asked sadly.

"When will you think you'll do what I asked?"

"Call me back this evening after 5."

"Okay Beautiful. Thanks for all your help."

"Don't mention it. By the way Chips, please be careful and safe."

"You too baby girl."

I got off the phone with Nakesha around the same time that my stomach growled for attention. Sleaze went out to get something to eat. While he was gone I was trying to formulate a plan. About 3 minutes before Sleaze got back I went into the bathroom to brush my teeth. On the way out of the bathroom I saw our door opening up. It wasn't Sleaze who had opened it!! It was the housekeeper!! She stopped in her tracks when she saw me. The look in her eyes told me that she saw my picture on the news. Out in the hallway I heard another housekeeper's voice. The partner came to see what caused her partner to stop at the door and freeze. She looked in at me and froze her damn self. That's when Sleaze appeared behind them and shoved them into the room. I put my finger to my mouth in the shush gesture. Sleaze closed the door but remained outside. When he came back in minutes later I asked him what he did and he told me that he pushed the carts around the corner into a utility room. We packed the guns into a bag and tied the women up with the phone and cable cords.

My first thought was to kill the housekeepers. Sleaze brought me to my senses reminding me that my heart is bigger than killing innocent people. So we secured them and got up outta there. We made it safely to the car without being seen by anybody else. We hopped in and headed back to the heart of the city. When we got off the expressway on Deerfield there was a roadblock with 3 city cops doing registration checks. I knew that that was only a ploy so the police can examine the occupants in the cars. We were the fourth car in line and we watched as the first 2 cars barely got looked at. The driver of those cars were white people!! The driver before us black but it was a woman. I guess that a signal was made indicating that our car had 2 black men in it because when we got close another cop had positioned himself opposite the cop that was actually looking at the cars because that didn't happen with the 3 cars before us. As soon as Sleaze stopped, the cop that placed himself on my side had placed his hand on his firearm. I had my window down already and my seat reclined. When the cop on my side made eye contact with me I raised my burner and pushed his wig loose!! I watched as his head snapped back and his body fell against his motorcycle. The cop on Sleaze side was slow to react. He fumbled with the button that housed his weapon and his slow reaction caused him his life. Sleaze raised his hammer and shot the cop in the upper chest; just above the vest line. The cop grabbed at his neck as he fell to the ground crawling, trying to get to his squad car. Sleaze didn't speed off like I thought he'd do. He just sat there and watched the other cop in the squad car for a minute. Just as Sleaze hoped would happen, did happen. The cop in the car got out to try to assist his partner. I raised myself out of the window and lent over the roof of the car and let off about 20 shots from the calico. I'm not sure if I connected or not but I created enough time for us to spin out before backup showed up. Sleaze drove to Grider and turned left heading towards the Hospital. The hospital wasn't our destination but that's where we ended up turning. The reason for us turning there was because it seemed like the whole police force was fast approaching from Delavan. The hospital grounds was our only option unless we committed suicide by crashing into a car head on. You must be able to tell that I'm not a crash dummy. We rather bang it out!!

When we turned into the parking area we thought that we were undetected. We were completely wrong. The security of the hospital heard over their radio that we had just had a shootout with the police and they were patrolling the grounds just in case we did come there.

Within A Week

The hospital cameras picked us up and the security team watching the cameras had radioed the patrol team of our whereabouts. We had parked in the back of the hospital hoping we were safe there for a while. We jumped out of the car and grabbed our cache of guns. Of course Sleaze smiled at me and said, "I'm gonna use the M-1 again bruh."

I smiled back and said, "have a blast!!"

"I guess this is it huh man?"

"I suppose so. Sorry it has to end like this bruh. You a good dude Sleaze. If it's Heaven or Hell we're off to, let's hook back up."

"Don't be sorry bruh. I had fun. It's been a great ride. The ending will be hella sweet!! I love you bruh!!"

"I love you more. Let's give these devils something to remember us by," I said as I grabbed my machine gun and turned it to fully auto.

CHAPTER 34

Special agent Licass, detectives Denardo & Bickford were exercising their own roadblock on the corner of Grider & Ferry. When they heard the desperate calls for help over the walkie-talkies they abandoned their post and headed towards the downed officers. Getting to the corner of Delavan & Grider they heard dispatch say that the suspects are on the Hospitals grounds. They were happy to hear that shit because they were only seconds away. They saw a few hospital security and Buffalo police speeding in that direction. Licass was driving and he passed the civilians entrance went directly to the entrance for the personnel and was immediately let in by the security manning the entrance. Upon entering he chose to go the opposite direction that the other official vehicles went. Detective Bickford asked, "You're going away from the action. Why is that?"

"Trust me, we're going in the right direction for the action."

"How do you know?"

Licass pointed his finger to a corner that had several ambulances and other medical vehicles parked. Sitting deep in the corner was our car sitting like a welcome mat at the door. Licass said, "that my friends will be the killers car!!"

"I'll be damned," said Denardo.

Licass said, "I want these fuckers alive if possible. Be careful because you know like I know that these niggers are playing for keeps and have nothing to lose."

Within A Week

Using the term niggers to describe the suspects had threw the detectives off a bit. They figured the FBI agent to be an asshole but not a racist one.

Licass pulled over and got out of the car. The detectives were about to report their location but Licass stopped them saying, "this is a huge opportunity for us. If we're able to nail these niggers ourselves we'll be promoted and given the keys to the city. Hell, we might even get to have dinner with that nigger Obama."

The idea was appealing to the 2 young detectives. Making this arrest would be really big for their careers. The young cops weren't naive to believe that they'll just walk right up and make an arrest. Bickford said, "Sir, are you forgetting that these men have killed people and officers? Did you forget the reason you were called in is because they're dealing with explosives? I highly doubt that they'll wave a white flag and surrender."

Licass heard him but he ignored him and opened his trunk to reveal a arsenal of weapons. He had military submachine guns, AR-15's, tech 9's, compact ouzi's and multiple versions of shotguns and handguns. Licass grabbed an AR-15 and 2 extra clips that held 30 rounds in each. After arming themselves with their weapons, they headed in our direction.

* * * * *

Somehow a news channel had overheard the events that were taking place because a news copter hovering in the sky almost directly above our position. The chopper seemed to be looking for us because it kept swaying. We lit up a dutch and waited for the beginning to the end.

At first I thought my mind was playing tricks on me or the sun had created shadowy figures crouching because I thought that I saw 2 or 3 devils trying to creep on us. I pointed in the direction I thought I saw the creepers and told Sleaze to send a grenade over there. Sleaze was all too happy to oblige. He aimed in that direction and fired. He hit a car and the explosion was loud and vicious. The explosion caused 2 other cars to explode also. The explosion scared off the creeping devils because they ran like hell to get away from it. I tried to stop them from getting far; I opened up fire in their direction. Shell casings got to poppin as my gun went off at rapid fire. My K-Cutter was ripping through cars and anything else in its path. As i was trying to down the cops, Sleaze was trying to down the helicopter overhead. All the gunfire had told our whereabouts and the area was soon filled with Buffalo's finest. Cops in cars and on foot were coming in our direction. Before long it was about 30 cops scattered everywhere in the parking lot hiding behind vehicles. Sleaze ripped off another grenade and hit a cop car killing several that were in the general area. Three cops tried to sneak up on us from the back but for some reason I looked in that direction and sprayed their ass with round after uncontrollable round. Cops were everywhere and shooting from all directions. My double vest was getting hit rapidly but the shells didn't penetrate. Sleaze was performing like a wildman!! It's like he was busting that M1 at high speed. The parking lot was like a scene from a movie. Cars were burning and turned over. Bodies and body parts were strewn all over the place. The cops that were living were running, ducking, hiding and trying not to be in any line of fire. Some of their tactics were awarded while others died for their efforts. Sleaze caught a copper in the head and the round went right through him and punched the cop behind him in the head.

I was letting off rounds when I heard Sleaze yell!! He fell to the ground and the M1 fell from his grasp. I ran to his side and saw a gaping shoulder wound. Sleaze abandoned the M1 and pulled out a pistol. We looked each other in the eyes and stood back up to continue trying to murder as many coppers as we could. It looked like we didn't kill any cops because the parking lot was filled with them devils. Our ammo was getting short while their crew was getting deeper. All that didn't matter though because I kept my K-Cutter on full tilt. Before long it seemed like I was busting alone. I looked over in the direction that I knew Sleaze was and saw nothing. I started panicking and forgot about the cops to run over where I saw Sleaze last. Behind a car is where I found Sleaze leaning against it. I was guessing that his shoulder was disturbing him but I looked closer and saw another gaping wound on his side where his vest wasn't protecting his body. He was sitting in a pool of blood. I looked up from the blood and watched as Sleaze took his final breath!! My pain ran so deep that I found it hard to breathe and I began to hyperventilate to the point of passing out.

CHAPTER 35

I awakened handcuffed to a hospital bed. There were 2 cops and a plain clothed detective sitting in my room. My body was aching and my mouth was parched & dry. I wanted water so badly. I tried to sit up but I was shackled to the fullest. Not only was my body aching, I must've gotten hit in the head because my head was heavily wrapped and I also had a cast on my arm and in a sling. The detective saw me stirring and came over to my bed. He looked down on me and told the 2 policemen to go have a break. When the cops left 2 more detectives came into the room. The head detective came to the bed and said, "Chester Chambers, you have the right to remain silent…" Before he was able to finish I cut him off, "save dat bullshit. Who the fuck is you?"

"I'm Special Agent Licass of the Buffalo Field Office of the FBI."

"What the fuck you want?"

"You're a very important man Mr. Chambers."

"That's not new. Tell me something I don't know."

"Okay, do you know that you're under arrest for at least 25 murders this past week?"

"Can I have something to drink?"

"Sure…. Nurse!!" Agent Licass yelled.

"Did you say 25 murders?"

"At the least. Give or take."

"If you don't get the fuck outta my face you'll be 26… Give or take!!"

"Tough man you are Mr. Chambers. I'll leave you for now. We'll talk soon enough." Agent Licass looked at the other 2 detectives and said, "C'mon gentlemen, let's allow this killer some rest. He's gonna need it."

After they left out the 2 uniforms came back in. The nurse came in with my drink right behind them. Just a few swallows was like a breath of fresh air. I went back to sleep trying to recall how I ended up here.

SEVERAL WEEKS LATER

I was reprimanded to a Federal Holding Facility located on the outskirts of Buffalo. I was still in a cast and kinda sore so they held me in the hospital ward of the jail. Somehow I've become an overnight celebrity. I was getting all kinds of fan mail and visit requests. I did accept one particular visit and that was from my lawyer; Leisha Scott. My lawyer was fine as fuck and very smart. She was assigned to me by the courts. I've learned that she requested me for her client. For some reason she found my case to be beneficial for her career. She would get the exposure and she felt that she was able to really help me. I could've hired myself a top-notch attorney but I liked Ms. Scotts spunk, beauty and aggression against the law. I wish that my case was winnable so that her debut was a victorious one!!

"Mr. Chambers are you ready to see your lawyer?" Asked the deputy.

"Just about. Let me gather up my legal work."

The deputy left for 3 minutes and came back to escort me downstairs to where my beautiful attorney awaited me. Upon entering the room I blessed Ms. Scott with my dazzling smile. She blushed and returned my smile with one of her own dazzling smiles. We've been sharing tiny intimate gestures ever since we've met. I think if things were under a different light I'd be able to bag her. I took the seat across from her and said, "Morning Beautiful, you look lovely as usual."

"Good morning Mr. Chambers. How are you this morning?"

"Please call me Chips."

"Fine. Call me Leisha."

"Alright Leisha. You win."

"Thank you Chips. We have a court appearance tomorrow for the discovery."

I've been trying to find a way to say this to her so I just said it outright. "Listen Leisha, I know that you wanna go through all the formalities that you were taught in school. I know you wanna get yourself some experience and exposure in the courtroom but this really isn't the case for that. I do have a case for you that you may find a bit more intriguing."

"Really? What would that case be?"

"I'll present it to you soon enough."

"So what now? Do we not discuss your current case?"

"Let's put my current case on the back burner. Go home and enjoy your day."

"If you say so. We'll still have to appear in court tomorrow. After that is over I'll see you in a week or two."

"Fine. See you tomorrow."

I had a trick up my sleeves. I never shared with my lawyer my reasons for flipping out. Yesterday I had to go to the infirmary. I asked them to take my blood and do some bloodwork. I was told that the results of my tests would be back in about 2 days. I'm 99.9% sure that my blood work will come back negative for Cancer. If I had that shit I would've been dead weeks ago. Not to mention, I can feel my body getting stronger with each passing day. I'll give Leisha Scott that info for her to pursue legally. I'm sure that we'll be able to sue the government amongst others for giving false information. Had I not been told that I had Cancer and was gonna die within a week, I wouldn't have gone and flipped my wig like I did.

Yesterday before my blood drawing I had received a letter from my favorite nurse; Nurse Nakesha. The letter read as follow:

"Dear Chips, hello handsome, how are you? I do pray that this letter finds you well and healthy. I'm fine myself. Things could be better and I'm sure that things will get greater later. I'm really sorry for your situation Chips. I know that in my heart you're a great guy. You're far the monster that the media has portrayed you to be. I'm not gonna get into any of that bullcrap though. I want you to know that I'll be here for you. I'll be your rock for however long you need me to be.

Now that I got that outta the way, remember several weeks ago you asked me if your dad was in the hospital? Well, had you called back you would've learned that your dad was indeed a patient at the hospital. He was admitted for an auto accident. He got hit by a van the day after you were admitted. ECMC must've ruined or just made a mistake and thrown your chart out by mistake and gotten yours and your father's blood results mixed up. Which brings me to this; as of yesterday your father was still on our Cancer floor where he passed this morning. I'm sorry to have to tell you in a letter like this. He fought hard for his life but the Cancer took its toll. His body couldn't fight it anymore. I'm sorry Chips.

Daddy, I know that you're fighting for your life but I think you should have your lawyer place a civil lawsuit against the Hospital and its entire chief of staff. I'm not sure what you will be able to title the lawsuit but there's negligence and delivering false information. That's of course if you're Cancer free. I also think it'll help in your defense somehow. I'll even be a witness against the Hospital. I've secretly copied yours and your files from the computer. Have your lawyer reach me and I'll give her everything I have.

Well handsome, although the news wasn't good news, I did enjoy writing to you. Hopefully I'll get to see you sooner than later. Until I see your handsome face again Chips take care and stay strong.

 LOVE, Nakesha B.

CHAPTER 36

The following morning I received some jailhouse mail. It said that I'm disease free. I had a clear bill of health and the chance to donate blood or my organs. Ain't that a bitch?! Here it is these devils wanna put me to death but before they do they wanna strip me for my body parts!! These devils are something else.

After reading the results from my tests I immediately called my attorney, Leisha Scott and sent her to meet Nurse Nakesha. I wanted to get her going for the lawsuit like yesterday. When I finished that task I fell into my daily workout routine. I was given by the doctors I could start doing light workouts. I wanted to stay fit; especially where I was and most likely heading. I've heard of many death threats already. I've killed niggaz cousins, brothers, sisters, dads, uncles and friends. It's only right that some of these niggaz want revenge.

* * * * *

I was cleared for general population-Finally!! They offered me PC but of course I turned that shit down. I've been waiting for this day. I was placed in cell 2 of G-Block. I was welcomed there with open arms. I ran into a few real niggaz that I haven't seen in years. A few cells from mine was my nigga Blade's. Blade was from a different hood but he and I were real cool. He used to cop work from me. Come to think of it, he still owed me for Bigg of soft!!

Within A Week

Anyway, when Blade saw me he smiled and came to my cell to greet me with a hug, cosmetics, food and some stamps. After sitting the items on my bunk he said, "My nigga Chips, this isn't where I'd rather see you but I'm glad to see you my dude. Sorry to hear about your situation bruh. Just know that I got yo back every step of the way." Blade then produced a dutch and sparked it up. After we got high as hell we sat at one of the tables on the block and kicked it. I was so high and caught up with kickin it with Blade that I didn't notice a dude walking by me with the mad ice grill. Blade knew the nigga and what the ice grill was about so he told me to follow him to his cell. At his cell Blade pulled out a long sharp banger. He gave it to me and showed me another one. We were strapped with twin bangers. Tucking the bangers we left Blade's cell and went to someone else's cell. The cell we went to was a nigga named Drew's cell. Drew was Money Mike's cousin. Drew got the word that I had knocked off his cousin and a few of his homies. Drew was one of those niggaz that was whispering death threats against me. Speaking on it was Drew's first problem. Everytime my situation came on TV he started yapping his mug. His second problem was he didn't know I wasn't no walk over. Everytime Drew opened his mouth about me, Blade just sat back and peeped shit.

Entering Drew's cell, Blade said, "Drew, this is Chips. You had a lot of shit about him on when he appeared on the News. Here he is."

Drew looked at Blade and said, "you funny as hell Blade."

Blade smiled and said, "Nah my man, yo ass funny as hell. You was just in front of the TV screaming all that murder, death, kill shit. The nigga you was speaking that shit about is standing in front of you and now you have nothing to say? You Pussy bruh!!"

I looked in the nigga Drew eyes and seen that he didn't want too but he swung on Blade. Blade was more shocked than hurt. Blade grabbed him and viciously slammed Drew on the cement floor. They tussled for 3 seconds before I pulled out my banger and went to work!! I sliced Drew in the face as Blade grabbed ahold of his legs as I started stabbing him repeatedly. I didn't count how many times I hit him but my arms were tired when I was done. The nigga didn't die but he was real fucked up!! I later learned that he got stabbed 42 times!! How the fuck didn't he die?"

I was on G-Block for less than 2 hours and had caught another case!! I was taken to the hole and was given 450 days there!! I'm sharing this shit with you right now from the hole!!

CHAPTER 37

The hole is a real piece of shit to be doing time. I never thought I'd find myself in this position. It's nothing though. I'm built tougher than these bars!! I've established myself a routine instead of just reading and staring at the walls in silence. Breakfast comes around 7am. I'll shit out the nasty food and workout until lunch comes around 11am. After lunch I'll shower and relax for several hours to let my muscles heal. I'll nap until dinner comes around 5pm and soon after the regular mail arrives. Once mails here I'll read all my fan mail and respond to selective letters. When I'm done writing letters I'm usually writing in this journal giving y'all the real deal or on the gate kickin it with my nigga Blade who just so happens to be in the cell next to mine. Yeah, life is pretty fucked up right now but it is what it is.

On this particular day a wrench was thrown into the game. During my morning workout I was interrupted by a deputy saying, "Chambers you have someone here to visit your lowlife ass!! Be ready in a half hour." I jumped up off the floor and got in the shower (showers are in our cells) After the shower I put on a fresh pair of jail issues and tossed my razor in my mouth.

Before I tell you who came to see me, let me explain the razorblade in the mouth. After Blade and I did that nigga Drew dirty, his peoples felt a certain way. They tried to get at Blade in the inmates visiting wait room. Blade told me that 3 fool boyz had tried him but wasn't aware or prepared for the razor that Blade spit from his mouth. The first nigga ran up and Blade sliced his ass from the top of his left eye all the way down to the left side of his chin. That nigga required 200 stitches & staples to close up his wound. He even lost an eye!! Blade stay clowning, referring to the nigga who lost his eye as 'Left Eye'. When the other 2 niggaz saw their homies eye ball on the floor, they changed their minds about continuing the attack. Blade told me that the situation didn't stop there. The person who came to see him was someone he didn't know!! It turned out that the person who set up the visit was Drew's brother & sister. Needless to say that Drew's brother & sister almost got their ass chopped up too. Luckily for them a deputy recognized Drew's brother from his many visits to Drew!!

Because of that incident, the inmates are let known who the person or persons that's coming to visit you. On this particular day it was my niggaz Gator & Dawg coming to see me. I was excited to see my niggaz. Everything went smoothly in the waiting room and when I walked into the visit room Gator & Dawg were seated at a table looking like straight drug dealers. Gator was rocking a pair of expensive jeans, a fly button up shirt with a pair of Mauri shoes. His chain was hanging near his belt buckle. His Rolex was glistening to set off the big stones in his ears. Dawg was wearing the same get up but in different colors. They looked like they had just come from the barbershop. I walked up and embraced them tightly. Of course Dawg being the loud nigga that he was said, "Damn Sun, look at you getting all buffed on a nigga. How are you doing?"

I just smiled and said, "I'm good my dude. I see life is treating you well."

"Life has no choice. I'd snatch life right from life if it didn't treat me well!!"

I smiled and looked at Gator and said, "How you bruh?"

"Regular. I'm just trying to keep 2 fools in check and stay outta way of all haters."

I looked puzzled for a second and then asked, "2 fools?"

"Yeah. This nigga here and Black crazy ass."

"Word? What's going on with Black?"

Within A Week

"Everything is going on with him!! He doesn't trust anybody outside of us three right here."

"What's wrong with that?"

"Money is what's wrong with that. Some of our faithfuls have been settling for lesser quality of bud because Black is wildin out on everybody that comes through. The other day the lil nigga shot up some nigga shit because he thought it was that nigga Damage."

I smiled at hearing that part. I liked the fact that Black was still repping me out there. I didn't like the fact that he was fucking up Gator & Dawg's bread up though. Not only that, I thought he'd learn a few things from and move differently because if he didn't he'd only end up dead or in a cell across from mine. I didn't want that for him. That's why I let him go on the fateful day that Sleaze got killed. I said to Gator, "please keep him out of harm's way. He look up to y'all and respect y'all. I'm gonna bless him with some bread soon and I need him out there and alive to get it."

"I got you Chips. The lil nigga gon be fine."

"That's what's up. How's the hood?"

Talking about the hood and excitement was Dawg's specialty. He said, "Sun, the hood is crazy as fuck!! The feds are coming through damn near everyday!! That cracker Licass still has a hard-on for me," exclaimed Dawg.

"You can't blame that devil Licass for trying to get you. You knocked off 2 pieces of shit and he knows you did it but can't prove it. Fuck him though. I almost got his ass that day."

"I wish you could've knocked his head off Sun!! Did you know that that shootout was live for a minute?" Dawg asked.

"Yo ass lying bruh!! Are you serious?"

Gator replied, "hell yeah it was. We watched it at Dawg's building."

"Say word bruh."

"Word Sun. That shit was mad wild!!"

"Where was the cameraman?"

"A helicopter captured it." Gator said.

"Yeah... The helicopter picked y'all up in the parking lot. It showed how Sleaze try to blow it outta the sky. That nigga was wildin that day!! I can only imagine if he and Zack were able to put it down together!! RIP to both of them."

Gator said, "I don't even wanna imagine that at all."

I said, "The world would be in trouble had them 2 niggaz was to link up."

Dawg said somberly, "We even saw when Sleaze went down Sun. That shit hurt my heart. I wish y'all could've knocked all them devils off. I wanted to ride up there and join y'all."

"We even saw when you went down Chips. We thought it was over for you too. I'm glad that the devils didn't finish you," Gator said.

"Listen y'all, I rather them devils had ended my life. The life I'm living now and facing isn't fit for an animal. I kinda wish that I did have Cancer. Speaking of Cancer, I got a big lawsuit in the makings. I'm gonna make you my trustee Gator. My lawyer will be getting in touch with you sometime this week. Also tell Black that he has 2 keys to 2 of my spots. I'll be sending him a kite to Hurlock this week so be on the lookout for it." I got up and embraced them; ending our visit. I enjoyed seeing them niggaz. I was happy they were still living life but I was saddened at the same time due to all the misery in which I was living and facing.

I headed to the strip search room and dropped my razor on the floor before entering it. I did swallow the balloon full of that Pineapple Express that Dawg had slipped me. Knowing that I'll be lifted off that bomb bud made me forget about my misery.

CHAPTER 38

In the hole, my cell and Blade's cell weren't within arms length of each other. We were on a block that held 8 cells. It was 4 on each side. Each cell was a cell length apart. Passing anything to Blade wasn't easy. I had to have a deputy or a trustee pass anything to Blade for me. For lunch we had mashed potatoes and chicken with a roll. The deputy that was serving wasn't a by-the-book type of officer. He came to put in his hours and not fuck with the people that already had misery. He slid my try into the slot in my door and moved on to the next cell. While he was serving Blade I put some of that piff up under the mashed potatoes and yelled for the deputy to come grab my try and give it to Blade. The cop did as I asked and Blade told me that he got the potatoes and he'll holla at me later.

Several hours later after we smoked we got on the gate and started talking. I shared with him how my visit with my niggaz was and the fact that my little nigga Black was still out there wildin out. Then I told him about Dawg seeing Sleaze and my last minutes together. Blade said to me, "fam, I saw that shit too!! That shit was like watching a movie. Especially when ya man raised that machine gun to the sky and started poppin that thing. Y'all niggaz was trying to go out with a bang for real. Seeing dude blow up a few cars with that grenade launcher blew my mind. On some real shit Chips, I thought y'all were some Arabs gone crazy!! When I learnt it was you; it broke my heart bruh. I was trying to figure out what led to that. You've always been a really cool dude. I never would've thought you'd be in here for the crimes that you're in here for."

"I know what you mean Blade. Shit is really fucked up. I never thought I'd be in here for the shit I'm in for. I thought maybe drugs; but multiple murders?! Never thought about it."

"Can I ask what happened?" Blade asked.

"Man, all this shit started when I got hit by that car. I went to the hospital for a few cracked ribs. Everything there was routine until the day I was supposed to be released." I fell silent thinking about that morning.

"What happened on that day?"

"The doctor came in with some bullshit papers saying that I couldn't leave because I had within a week to live."

"Damn yo; for real? Why did the doctor tell you that?"

"He told me that I have fatal Cancer and I'll die from it within a week."

"Damn bruh, that's fucked up. How long has it been?"

"It's been well past a week!!"

"So how did you get caught up with all this murder shit?"

"I kinda believed what the doctors said and I gave up on life. I said fuck it!! I chose to turn it up instead of tone it down."

"I probably would've done the same in that position. There was nothing to live for."

"Yeah, my man Sleaze was already a live wire and I figured that we can turn up and I could leave him crazy paid. Shit was going according to plan until a few niggaz got out of line. When I knocked off the first 3 clowns it stirred something inside me and I began viewing every nigga that wasn't down with me as clowns and I couldn't stop puttin niggaz heads to bed."

Blade and I talked until the wee hours of the night. We paused after shift changes just to smoke some more Pineapple. We didn't talk anymore murder shit though. We just did a lot of laughing and talking about some of the bullshit we've been through and some of

Within A Week

the Monkeys we've ran through. Blade was a real cool dude. I really liked him. Luckily for him he'll be going home one day. I decided that when Blade did touch down I was gonna have Black look out for him.

CHAPTER 39

The following morning after breakfast I smoked and deaded my normal workout routine. Instead, I smoked and enjoyed my high. Blade came to his gate to toss it up some more. He gave me his life story. He told me that he's from Central Park(CP). He's real close to a few real niggaz I know from over that way. My love for Blade only grew deeper. We talked until lunch came. After lunch was over I tried to get some rest. I was allowed about 30 minutes of relaxing before I was interrupted by a knock on my cell door. I rubbed my eyes and focused on the face that was staring in at me. The face was a face that I've seen before but couldn't place where. The face was that of a beautiful black Monkey. I mean this Monkey was fine as fuck!! I jumped out of the bunk and rushed to the cell door. I squatted to the tray slot and was greeted with some thick thighs and a fat pussy print. I immediately put on my smile and said, "hey beautiful, how and who are you?"

"My name isn't Beautiful. It's Ms. Jacobs. I'm new here and I'll be the officer working in this unit."

"Okay, that's what's up. I'm Chips. Why'd you knock on my cell door?"

"I wanted to see the infamous Chester Chambers."

"Sounds like you may be a fan."

"Who knows?"

"If that's the case, don't keep it a secret too long. Holla at me."

"Maybe I will….. When the time is right."

That Monkey made my day more interesting. When I was talking to her I had the feeling that I talked to her before but couldn't grasp where or when. Whatever... I'm gonna go at that deputy while she's working this block. I have nothing to lose and everything to gain.

* * * * *

It was hard for Chelsea Jacobs to maintain her composure while talking to Chips. She wanted to kill him the very first moment she saw him. She knew that she had to keep a cool head if her plan to have him murdered work. She had to play the role of an officer that was down for Chips best interest.

Chelsea is the baby mother of Big Rob. When the police interviewed her after Big Rob's murder they never knew that she was a federal corrections officer in training. Having Chips in her place of employment wasn't her doing or idea but it was a plus that he was there. Her only doing was requesting to move from her location to the hole. Once her switch was rewarded she devised a plan to have Chips murdered for killing her baby's father. She was thrilled that Chips hadn't recognized her and his interest in her was outside the officer inmate realm. She felt that all her plans were gonna work to a tee.

* * * * *

Seeing that fat ass walk away from my cell turned me on. Her ass was Phat!! I was definitely feeling shorty for real. Had I ran into her in the streets she would've been bagged and tagged without a doubt. I'm gonna go hard at shorty. She's gonna hit me with some of that pussy. I saw it in her eyes. She's gonna go for my charm or my bread. Either way, we gon fuck!!

Ms. Jacobs stopped at Blades cell and chatted with him for a few minutes. When she left the tier Blade called down to me and said, "Chips, did you see that fatty? She is a cutie too!!"

"Hell yeah I saw that fatty. She can definitely get it. I'm gonna work on that Monkey every chance I get."

"I feel you on that my nigga. It seemed like she was digging you too bruh!!"

I bolstered my cockiness and said, "all hoes dig me!! On some real shit Blade, I think I know shorty from somewhere. I just can't place it yet."

"It be like that when you run through mad hoes. You tend to forget a few in the shuffle."

"Nah bruh, that's not it. She got something special about her."

"There's something definitely special about her.. That Ass!! Blade said while laughing.

CHAPTER 40

The following morning I was working out when Ms. Jacobs came to my cell and said, "good morning handsome."

"Handsome? Well good morning to you also; Sexy!!"

"How was your night? Did you sleep well?"

"Aside from all the tossing and turning; I slept well."

"Good for you."

"Why did you say it like that?"

"It's just that I'm single and I hate sleeping alone. There's no fun in that."

"Single? Why would a beautiful woman like yourself be single?"

"Yep… Single as a dollar bill. I'm single by force but that's another story."

"Don't tell me that dudes are afraid of a woman in uniform?"

"We won't get into any of that but Dudes be trying. I will say that most of the good men are either dead or in jail."

"With me being here, I can agree with that assessment." I agreed with her.

While she stood at my cell talking, I heard over the walkie talkie that I have a visit scheduled for a half hour from now. She took a few steps back so that I wouldn't hear the next exchange of conversation. After she cleared her conversation she came back and said, "well player, you have a visit from a Nakesha something or other. I'll be back to get you in 20 minutes." She said with some fire in her voice.

On the way to the visiting room deputy Jacobs asked, "so, is this your woman coming to see you?"

"That would be my business wouldn't it? Just to answer your question though, no it's not."

"I apologize for prying."

"Don't be sorry. Just try not inquiring into my personal life please."

"Cool Mr. Chambers."

"We're back to Mr. Chambers huh?"

"Always have been." She said as we reached the visit room. "Have a good visit Mr. Chambers."

There was only about 6 other niggaz waiting for a visit. I scanned the whole area and noticed 1 nigga jive watching me. I caught him watching me so I stepped to him asking, "my man, do you know me or something?"

"Nah. Why do you ask that?"

"I look around and when I look in your direction I see you watching me. Do we have issues of some kind?"

"Nah dude, it ain't like that."

I stepped to the other side of the room and put my back to the wall and stilled myself to study the fool that was watching me. Then it hit me like a sledgehammer; this was one of the niggaz that was chillin with Drew!! My first thought was to spit out my razor and ox his ass down. Then a better thought came to mind. I decided to have Nakesha learn who his visitor was and befriend them.

My visit with Nakesha was all good. She had told me that she met up with my lawyer over coffee. She gave my lawyer my dad's and my charts that she copied. I told Nakesha about the clown that was with Drew. I pointed him out to her and had her make it possible so that him and I will be in the waiting room together again. When the visit was over I held Nakesha very tightly and gripped her juicy ass. She slipped her tongue into my mouth and to my surprise she inserted a balloon full of that piff!!

* * * * *

Within A Week

"I see that you had a good visit with your so-called friend. To me it looked more than just a friend visit," Deputy Jacobs said.

"Hold up officer... What is it with you? Why are you on me the way are? Do you have some ill feelings toward me or is it infatuation speaking?"

"Chips. I mean Mr. Chambers, I think Stevie Wonder has better vision than you."

"I guess he would with all the smoke screen blocking my vision."

"Smoke screen? I'm putting my career at risk by showing you my interest in you."

"I can see there's some interest, I just can't figure the interest."

We were just about to enter the unit when she stopped us in a camera's blind spot and pushed her sweet tongue into my mouth!! I was taken by complete surprise. I hadn't even swallowed the loony that Nakesha had given me. Deputy Jacobs felt the balloon and asked me what it was. I pulled it out and showed her the balloon. She told me to put it in my socks and she came in for a deeper kiss!! I was surprised by her forwardness. I can't say that I understood her but it felt good. After the kiss we continued on to my cell. When I was locked in she told me that things will get greater later!! With that, she sashayed her sexy ass away from my cell. I won't lie, she had me off balance. She moved like a hood bitch would. I decided to get into her business before I got into her panties.

* * * * *

Chelsea walked away from Chips cell questioning herself. Was she really jealous of Chips visit with the other bitch? Was she stupid for kissing him and actually wanting more? Was she acting upon a high school crush? Should I report him for having that balloon full of drugs? She threw out all doubts and reasoned that everything she's doing is for the greater good. She told herself that she was doing things correctly in order to set Chips murdering ass up!! She decided to put herself out there further to gain his trust by taking him a lighter after she used the restroom. She went into the ladies room and pulled down her pants & thongs only to find to her dismay that she was wett as fuck!! She was amazed with how turned on she was behind his kiss. She sat down and urinated. The wipe caused her mind to go back to Chips kissing here and his firm grip on her waist and ass. Those thoughts had made her very horny. Without thought she started rubbing her clit furiously. Her fingers were putting her in a state of euphoria. She slid 2 fingers inside her pussy and creamed heavily as she came hard!! She gathered her wits and smiled at the mischief & lewdness she just displayed with her thinking. Her mind went further into her nasty thoughts. She chose not to wash her hands because she wanted to rub her fingers over Chips face so he can get a whiff of how her pussy smelled. Walking back down the block she stopped at Chips cell and called him to the cell door. She gave him the lighter and said, "this is for your smoke. You didn't get it from me and try not to get caught."

"Why are you doing this Ms. Jacobs?"

"Just take it and please stop asking questions."

I accepted the lighter and said, "thank you."

"Oh yeah, I have something else for you," she said as she reached 2 fingers to my nose.

"DAMN!! That's all you baby?"

"Who else would it be?"

"Yo pussy smell good as fuck!!"

"Do it? I thought you'd like a little buzz."

"Like it? I love it!! Too bad I can't have it live & direct."

"Cards have been dealt. You have the winning hand. Play your cards right and perhaps you can have it live & direct."

CHAPTER 41

When she left her pussy scent under my nose it ruined my whole day. I couldn't believe she held me like that!! I immediately started beating my dick!! It's been a long time since I've gone that route but I beat off 5 times. Everytime I inhaled, her pussy scent popped into my senses and it led to beating my dick. After I've worn myself out and came to complete exhaustion it dawned on me that she gave me a lighter also. I twisted up some good green and got high as hell!! When I was as high as the planes be it hit me that I had to write a kite to Gator to ask him to find out what he can about this Deputy Jacobs. This Monkey really has the best of me right now. She has me intrigued and spooked at the same time. I don't really know what to make of all her moves. I pulled out my writing pad & pen and formulated the words to Gator.

 My nigga G, what up bruh? How's the street treating you? I pray that all is well and you and the family are good. I'm cool as you already know. How's Black & Dawg doing? Tell them niggaz I said what up and to keep a cool head.

 Listen bruh, there's this Monkey that works here; she's a deputy and her last name is Jacobs. I need you to find out who she is. She is riding my dick hard as hell. She kissed me and fingered herself later just to come and put her pussy scent under my nose so I smell it!! It smelled good as fuck too!! I got hit with a loony and she gave me a lighter to lite up with. She even went to the point of telling me that if I play my cards right I'd be able to smash. The thing is this; I've seen this Monkey before. I'm sure that we've crossed paths out there. I just can't find it in my memory to where I know her from.

Anyhow bruh, I need you to make that happen like yesterday for me. She'll be off for the next 3 days and I'm hoping that you'd receive this kite and have the needed info ASAP. I really appreciate you dude. Hold ya head and stay out of the suckaz radars. You're my nigga until the end of time.......

Chips,
Box N Moe

After I finished that letter I rolled up another fatty and got higher as hell and got to kickin it with Blade. I told him in so many words what's been going on. He told me that he noticed how dept Jacobs was heavy at my cell. I sent him some more smoke and tossed it back and forth until I passed out!!

CHAPTER 42

The next 3 days went by relatively the same as any other day. However, the 3rd day, the day Ms. Jacobs came back to work was a different day altogether. It started as usual with breakfast being served. Once breakfast was over Ms. Jacobs strolled her fine ass up to my cell door and said, "hey good looking!! How've you been since the last time I saw you?"

"Hey Beautiful!! I've been coolin as usual. How've you been? Enjoy your days off?"

"I've been good. I did enjoy my days off."

"That's what's up. What did you enjoy about your days off?"

"I enjoyed not having to work and being able to relax. I will say this though, I did miss being here."

"Oh really? What did you miss about being here?"

"You," she said with a smile.

I smiled back my smile and realized that this Monkey just might be for real so I said, "I've missed you also. You left me beating off for the past few days."

"Oh really!? Too bad I couldn't watch you handling your business."

"If you play your cards right you'd catch me sooner than later."

We shared a few shit & giggles until her walkie-talkie interrupted us with, "Dep. Jacobs, inform Mr. Chambers that he has a visit in a half hour." She replied, "10-4." She looked at me and said, "you're very popular. I wonder who's coming to see you this time."

"Damn sweetheart, we were vibing very well and then you go worrying about the wrong things."

"I'm sorry.... Let me go so you can get ready. I'll be back in a few to take you down to your visit." She sashayed her fat ass away as I got ready to jump in the shower. Twenty minutes later Ms. Jacobs was back and ready to escort me to my visit. For some reason or other we were a bit late. She told me that my visitors are both male and one of them last name is Jackson. I knew then that it was Gator & Dawg coming to see me. Being that we were already late I didn't have to wait in the waiting room and was brought right to the dance floor. Gator & Dawg saw us entering and they both smiled. I walked up and slapped them up with a hug right after one another. Gator looked at me and said, "don't tell me that's the Monkey you wrote me about."

"Yeah, that's her. She looks familiar, right?"

Dawg looked and said, "she should look familiar Sun, she was a cheerleader at Park!!"

I looked and thought of those basketball days and said, "yo black ass is right Dawg!! That is her. The head cheerleader."

"She never told you bruh?" Asked Gator.

"Nah man, she never told me shit!!"

"When you get back ask her," said Dawg.

"It's no wonder she's been on my dick. She wanted me to hit it back in the day."

"Why didn't you hit it bruh?"

"I was too busy smashing all the other hoes. Besides, she wanted to be my main bitch and I wasn't having that shit."

"I guess y'all met up for a reason. You better hit that shit now Sun," Dawg said.

"You already know."

After we were done with that topic Gator said, "have you caught the news?"

"Nah... Why what happened?"

"Ya lil nigga Black is a real killer. I don't know what happened to him but he's a crazy muthafucka."

"Why, what happened?"

Within A Week

Dawg wanted to tell me in his animated way so he said, "Sun, the other day we were on the block doing what we do and who comes through? That nigga Damage and his cousin. They came for that Pineapple but we started talking and Damage mentioned your name."

"What did he have to say about me?"

"Nothing really... He just asked how you were doing!!"

"Dude was just asking how you were doing and Black asked him why. Before long words are being thrown around and Damage asked Black, 'do you know who the fuck I am?' Black replied with, 'yea... You're that pussy ass nigga Damage. The nigga who sent the 2 dead clowns to try to kill my mans Chips & Sleazy but ended up killing my boy Frog!! I know exactly who you are.' You already know that I'm around for all the bullshit so I stepped up and said, 'Sun, is that true? You got my lil nigga Frog clipped?' The nigga was backing up to his car as he was talking and jumped in that bitch quickly. Before we knew it, we heard tires screeching!! No sooner after that, all I heard was Blacks cannon going off. His joint caused a chain reaction and 3 or 4 more burners got to popping!!"

"Word? Anybody get touched?"

"Hell yeah Sun!! Damage cousin Shells got hit up like 6 times!! On the news they said that he's in stable but critical condition. The block has been on edge since then. The Feds keep coming through trying to find shit out. We shut the spot down and have been laying low," said Dawg.

"Damn, I wish I was out there to get it poppin. Tell Black to chill though."

"Bruh, Black needs a full time hustle. He's either gonna kill somebody and become your cellmate or get his little ass knocked off," Gator retorted.

"Yea... You're right. I got something for him. I'm gonna send him a kite."

"I thought you did that already?" Asked Gator.

"I did. That was some other shit though."

"Alright, do that, put him on. If he stays on the block any longer we're gonna go broke and he's gonna get himself killed."

"I got him."

We ended our visit with another hug and handshake and Dawg hitting me with more bud!! Gator told me that he just put 3 stacks in my account!! I love them niggaz!!

CHAPTER 43

On the way back to my cell she stopped us again in the blindspot and grabbed my dick and kissed me deeply. My dick grew hard as steel and fast as fuck. I wanted to fuck her right then & there!! Pulling away from the kiss she dropped into a squatting position, freed my dick and simply kissed it!! She put my dick back inside my pants, stood back up and led the way back to my cell. I rushed into my cell and stripped down immediately and began beating off right in front of her. She was licking her lips the whole time watching me. That shit was mad exciting!! I bust off in less than 2 minutes!! My cum erupted out of my dick and flew to the spot where she was looking through the window.

"Damn Chips.... You bust off amazingly. I like that. I'm impressed."

"You haven't seen shit baby girl," I said with a smile.

"I think I've seen enough to know."

"Nah ma, you haven't seen shit. I bust off at that pussy like I used to shoot the ball in high school."

"You played ball in high school?"

"Yea... For the same team you cheered for in high school."

"What are you talking about?"

"You already know!! You cheered for me and wanted me back in school. I couldn't figure it out for a minute. I knew that I knew you from somewhere."

"Yea, that was me. How'd you find out?"

"Remember Gerald Jackson?"

"That name sounds familiar. Is he one of the guys that came to see you?"

"Yea. He saw you when you brought me down."

"How does he know me?"

"He fucks with an old friend of yours."

"What friend?"

"Andrea."

"For real? How is she doing?"

"She's good!! He takes real good care of her."

"What a small world!!"

"Why didn't you tell me about us knowing each other?"

"Don't really know."

"It would've eased my mind and made things flow smoother for us."

"Well, I gotta do a round. I really enjoyed the show you put on. If you keep playing your cards right things will get better."

"We'll see. I'll see you later."

* * * * *

Chelsea walked thinking if Chips that she was Big Rob's baby mother. She was nervous and afraid that her plans were gonna be destroyed. She made the decision right then that she was gonna have Chips clean the stairwell and give him some pussy!! She really wanted to fuck him but she made herself believe that it was all apart of her plan to get him murdered. After seeing him jerk off to her it made her pussy juice up with desire. She found it very difficult to stand in front of him talking while her pussy was throbbing for his dick. With her plan to fuck him in the sttairwell, she rushed to the restroom to get herself off with the image of him stroking her wet pussy.

After Chelsea had given herself an exhilarating orgasm, she was ready for some real dick pushing between her slick walls. She got the okay from her Sergeant to allow an inmate to clean the stairwell.

She rushed to Chip's cell and said, "Mr. Chambers would you mind doing a chore for me?"

He got up off his bunk and sat his book down as he replied, "sure, what is it? Should I get dressed for it?"

"You're dressed okay. I just need you to clean something for me," she said as she unlocked his cell.

After securing his cell she led him to the stairwell that lead to the outside rec area. Once the door clicked behind them she turned and faced him. She squatted before him and pulled his sweats down to his knees. She looked up at him as she pulled his boxers down and grabbed his dick and put it in her mouth. She worked his dick in her mouth for all of three minutes before he was extremely hard. She stood up and lowered her pants and thongs. She turned around and bent over saying, "I need to feel you deep inside me!! Fuck me Chips"

Chips grabbed the base of his dick and rubbed the head across her moist pussy lips to find her juicy and ready. He exhaled and said, "Damn Ms. Jacobs." He was cut off from his words by her saying, "Chelsea…. Call me Chelsea."

"Damn Chelsea, I've never had a pussy this wet before. I'm gonna fuck the dog shit outta you. First I gotta put some of that sweet juice on my moustache." He squatted down and buried his face in between her sexy ass cheeks. His nose was in her asshole as his mouth eagerly sucked up as much juice as her juicy pussy would allow. When he felt his face was smeared and her erotic juices invaded his senses he stood up and gripped her waist tightly. He grabbed his dick and pushed it against her soaking wet entrance and pushed himself deeply inside her. Chelsea moaned and gasped when she felt his heavy nut sack slap against her aroused clit. He stroked her hard and fast. It's been months since she felt some real meat inside of her and Chips was applying the right amount of pressure on her thirsty walls. After a few more strokes Chips felt her walls tighten around his dick and heard her cry out that she was cumming. Her clutch and cries took him over the edge and he bust the biggest nut in his life deep inside her.

Chelsea placed her hands on the wall to steady herself because that dick left her unsteady and off balance. He pulled his dick out of her only to find her dropping to her knees to clean him up with her mouth. He stood rigid as he said, "damn Chelsea, you got some bomb ass pussy and head. Too bad we didn't get together when I was a free man."

"Yeah… It is too bad."

"Everything cool Chelsea?"

"How could it not be cool? You got some real good dick!!"

Chips smiled and said, "glad you liked."

"Me too… C'mon, let's get you back before someone gets suspicious."

She took him back to his cell, locked him in and went back to her post. She ate her lunch thinking how good Chips put the dick on her and she can't wait to feel it again. However, revenge is a must!!!

CHAPTER 44

Chelsea arranged for her cousin Slump, who's convicted of two homocides already and is facing two more federal murder charges, who happens to be placed at the very same federal hold that she's working in; to be secured in the same block that Chips is housed in. In her mind, her plan was working beautifully. All she had to do was keep Chips with his pants down and she can easily have him murdered for killing her baby's father. Upon Slumps arrival she put him on point who the target is.

* * * * *

Officer Jacobs came down to my cell after she placed another nigga on the block. "Who is that kat?" I asked.

"Some dude that came down from state prison facing federal murder charges."

"Word? What's his name?"

"Byron Anthony."

"Where's he from?"

"Well damn, I came to kick it with you and you're asking 21 questions about this nigga."

"My bad Sexy, it's just that I like knowing who's in my vicinity. I have a gang full of enemies."

"I hear that. Can I ask you something?"

"Yea. What's up?"

"What happened to you? I mean, you were always such a good guy. How did you get into the situation you're facing?"

"I really don't know baby."

"Something changed because you were such a sweetheart, far from a bad boy."

"I'm still a sweetheart." I said with my killer smile.

"Your short answers indicate that you don't really wanna talk. I'll move along." She started to turn away and leave but I stopped her by saying, "hold up Beautiful." She stopped moving and turned back around. I inhaled and slowly let the air out before saying, "A few months ago I had this accident involving a car. I was taken to ECMC for treatment but ended up staying for a few days. Mainly for observation reasons. It's ironic that my father sustained a more serious accident the day after mine and he too was taken to ECMC. His injuries were parallel to mine. The Physicians fucked up when they ran the blood test."

"Wait, how'd they fuck up?"

"They fucked because they didn't cross their T's and dot their I's. My father and I share the same name. I'm a junior. Anyway, my father's blood work showed that he had Cancer. The Cancer he carried was untreatable."

"How did that have any affect on you though?"

"The effect it had on me was that the Doctors didn't tell my father he had within a week to live...... They told me that shit."

Tears sprang into Jacobs eyes. She then asked, "A week has gone by a long time ago."

"Absolutely. That statement was meant for my father's ears not mine. I was lied to and misled by the hospital's mistake."

"That doesn't justify all your crazy charges."

"Certain things happen within a person's mind when they think their lives don't have a future. That's what happened to me. My life mentally changed and the impact was greater than I even expected. Thinking that I only had within a week to live, I became less passive and crazy aggressive. The things I used to turn my head away from, I went head-on into it. I started thinking of all the people that took my

Within A Week

passiveness as a weakness and confronted them. Having that bullshit and false information changed me. Here I am."

"Can I ask about the so-called terrorist shit in the fruitbelt?"

"Well, there was a dude from that hood named Money Mike. I used to supply him with his work. One day I gave him some work and he decided to not pay me. He was influenced by some kat from over there name Big Rob. Big Rob in turn had some young kats so -call press me about supplying that hood with work when Big Rob had work for his hood. As I've said earlier, I turned my head from some shit and that was something I turned away from.

On the day I was released from the hospital after hearing that I had within a week to live, my lil nigga, the one who got killed by the police on the hospital grounds? Sleazy? Well Sleazy wanted to go over there and press for that owed paper. Sleazy has always been around for the bullshit. With Sleazy knowing my fate, he knew I was down for whatever. We got up with Money Mike and demanded the paper that's owed to me and we were gonna be gone without problems. Money Mike tried to play us and Sleazy popped his top. We found Money Mike's stash and took the money owed to me and Sleazy took the rest for his troubles. Later we learned that the money Sleazy took belonged to Big Rob. Big Rob could've done things differently and things would've turned out different but he sent some young goons to my block on some gangsta shit and got them goons killed. Being that Big Rob made such a malicious move against me, I had to get at him or he was gonna keep sending goons my way and Big Rob had an abundance of goons at his disposal. The Fruitbelt has been breeding killers since the 50's. I had to take out the head of the snake or them niggas would keep coming until I was dead. Ironic that I only had within a week to live anyway. I wasn't letting niggas kill mr though.

That whole terrorist shit was all jazzed up for the public's consumption. It was simply a nigga doing what he had to do for survival. If I could take this whole situation back I would."

Chelsea had tears in her eyes threatening to fall. She sniffed and very quietly said, "Damn, You really weren't just on some bullshit.

Things just turned to bullshit for you. It all started with the hospital fucking up."

"Exactly.... That's why my lawyer's are on Erie county as a whole. I have a huge lawsuit ongoing right now."

"Good for you. Listen handsome, I gotta go. I gotta do a round and get ready to go home. I'll see you tomorrow. Have a nice remainder of the day and dream about me," she said with a seductive smile as she sashayed her hips for Chips to see.

* * * * *

Chelsea had to hold back her tears as Chips explained to her how his position came to be. Her heart was hurting with confusion. The love of her life and the father of her child was murdered by her high school crush; the man she was catching true feelings for. She was in a fucked up state of mind and needed to think things through. Her order for Chips death remained a go.

CHAPTER 45

The next day began the same as every other day with the exception of our block having rec together. Usually we were given rec individually. Everyone attended rec except for myself and the new guy, which I learned was named Slump. I don't know why he didn't go but my reason for not going was because Officer Jacobs wanted me to stay back to do some "cleaning" for her. The "cleaning" I'm about to do for Jacobs had my mind reeling. She had some bomb pussy. It stayed gripping my dick as I stroked. Plus she can take some dick. I was hitting her with some of my best and deepest strokes and she just kept on pushing her pussy back at me. I can't wait to start "cleaning" for her.

While everyone was at rec I had rolled up some bomb buds and got high as a muthafucka. As I reached my highest state I layed back on my bunk and dozed off. During that brief state of sleep I had a nightmare that caused me to wake up drenched in sweat. I dreamed that I was the victim of all the murders I committed. I was Money Mike staring down the barrel of my burner. Then I was Big Rob being gunned down while begging for my life. I was Armstrong staring out the window as I pulled up next to his car and opened fire. I was the goons from Fruitbelt that experienced a Iraq-like bombing. I was the police that found their end on the Hospital grounds. I was the cops that got held up in the traffic jamb. The scariest part of my dream was when I turned into that bitch-ass FBI pussy, Agent Licass. When I was him, I felt the relentlessness he felt at pursuing me. Through his eyes I saw the shot that sat Sleazy down for good. Through him I watched in horror as he aimed his firearm and hit me up. I watched myself fall to never get up. In my nightmare I watched myself die a thousand deaths and killed a thousand times!!!

As I stood up I heard Blade knocking at my cell. He came to tell me that the Feds were moving him to another facility. Neither of us knew why this was happening. Then he reminded me that his time was short and his release will happen sooner than later. He passed me a piece of paper that contained his personal information. I took it and shook his hand at the same time saying, "keep it official bruh. Be sure you go check on my nigga Black when you touch down."

After Jacobs escorted Blade off the block she hightailed it back to my cell for some conversation. She really didn't have shit to say, she was more intent on asking questions. Being that I just woke up from that nightmare and I was still kinda high, I wasn't in a talkative mood. She sensed my mood and decided to make an excuse to leave. She bid me farewell until the next day.

I was glad she had left me alone. I had to toss a few things around in my head and I didn't need any form of distractions. One of the things I had to toss around was why would a fine as Officer risk her job for a nigga who has no hopes of ever coming home? It's not just the dick. Her ass is showing feelings. I gotta play her closely the next time I'm with her.

CHAPTER 46

Later that day I decided to drop my lil nigga Black a kite. I've been slacking with keeping up with the outside world because I was getting pussy inside. I needed to put Black on my ideas anyway. I put all things aside and let my thoughts pour onto the paper.

"Black, what's up lil homie? How're you doing? IO hope all is good and life is treating you well. You should already know that that I'm maintaining under the constant strain in which I'm living. I've been hearing about you out there reppin in the streets. Let me share something with you young player. Don't let busting your gun define who you are as a man. The real gangsta niggaz aren'y known as gangstaz. They're powerful business minded men who do dirt in silence. Money is the key to it all. The nicest whips, homes, clothes and jewels are gotten with that mighty dollar. Them bitches come with the money and cum for the money. However, more shit comes with the mighty dollar. Envy, hate, greed and jealousy is born and raised through OPP- Other People's Paper!! Pay attention out there because most niggaz carry those poisonous traits like bitches carry handbags. Do your numbers and steer clear of the limelight.

You don't know it but I'm a millionaire. I played hard and for keeps while I was running them streets. You didn't know it but you have the key to becoming that nigga out there. You just have to stay focused and move like a boss to a gangsta melody.

With that being said, there's 3 important keys on the ring with the car keys you have. One of the keys goes to my spot on Herman.

Go there and go in the basement. In a chest you'll find all kinds of weapons. Don't let the sight of them burners allow you to lose focus though. That spot is my low-key spot. Keep it as yours. The only people that know of that spot are me, you and Sleazy. Not one bitch ever been brought there. It's not a place for fun.

In the master bedroom beneath the floorboards up under the entertainment set is 15 bricks of raw and the Diamonds. Don't sell bricks bruh. Try to get rid of it all in ounces at a time. Sit on the diamonds for several months before you get rid of them.

There's also 100 bands under the old school car in the yard. The car will only go in reverse. A large piece of plywood is under it. Move the wood and dig there. The keys to the car are hanging on the keyboard next to the backdoor. I need you to put 25 bands a month in there for me. I'll be needing it for my defense and my stay here for however long that may be.

Another key goes to the spot on Hurlock. Gator has keys to it also. Use that spot to make your street moves. Give Gator the other key on the ring that goes to nothing I've mentioned. Situate yourself and come with Gator & Dawg to see me next week or so.

Until the end of time my lil nigga…. Stay safe and get money!!!

Chips…

After my letter to Black was done I fell back and rolled up another blunt. After my high came, I drifted off to sleep.

CHAPTER 47

When I awakened breakfast was being served. The same ole bullshit as usual. I ate the bread and drank the juice & milk. After breakfast was over I hit the floor and started my workout. Again, as usual I was interrupted by Officer Jacobs with her usual tapping at my door. I didn't mind the interruption this time. I looked up and she was sporting a beautiful smile as she said, "hey good lookin."

"Morning Sunshine... How're you this morning?"

"It's going good. Thanks for asking."

"Did you sleep well?"

"I slept well enough; thanks to you."

She smiled and asked, "oh yea, how'd I do that?"

"The way you vibe with me makes it comforting for me to relax."

"Is that so?"

"I thought of our encounter as I layed in bed."

"Did you do anything other than think?" She asked, searching if I beat off or not.

"Yea... I cashed a check and fell out like a baby."

"Cashed a check?"

"Yea... Can I ask why don't you have a man?"

"I believe I've told you already."

"No baby girl, you told me some bullshit."

"I told you the truth. Honestly."

"Do you have any shorties?"

"I have one son."

"Is his father in his life? Who is the dad if you don't mind me asking?"

"The who is irrelevant. His dad is in the grave."

"I'm sorry for your loss. You're not dating out there?"

"There were only two men I liked in that manner and one is dead and the other is in jail."

"Damn baby girl, your luck sounds just like mine; all bad."

"You can say that again."

"So what have you been doing since high school?"

"Got pregnant and living life as it's given."

"Am I prying too deeply? All your answers are kinda evasive."

"Sorry. I gotta go do my rounds. I'll be back later."

She bounced on me without a second glance. Something was definitely up with her but I couldn't put it together yet. Fuck it, I'll just keep fucking through her sexy ass until I do figure her out.

She was back twenty minutes later telling me that my lawyer was here to see me. I got dressed and was escorted to visit my lawyer. My lawyer just wanted to drop off some legal work for me to look over. I needed to tell my lawyer about the key Gator has and it goes to a lockbox that held over a million cash and Gator would contact her to give her 200k for her great work.

When I returned to my cell, Officer Jacobs told me that I missed rec and I'm eligible for make-up rec if I choose. I was gonna turn it down until she gave me that look that said I should take advantage of make-up rec. My dick took over the thinking and I took her advice and chose rec. She gave me twenty minutes before rec time so I can smoke and shit. While sitting on the toilet I addressed the letter to Black and stamped it.

Being that my case is so high profile and the Feds always rummaging through my incoming and outgoing mail, I use the white boy Dusty to send out any mail I wish to keep from the Feds. I hook the white boy up with some commissary for his help.

Officer Jacobs came back and unlocked my cell. Then she went to the stairwell door to wait for me. I came out and headed to Dusty's cell and gave him the mail I needed for him to send out and some food and smoke. I turned and headed towards Officer Jacobs and the stairwell door. She opened it and told me to wait just inside as she had to run to the control room to lock my door. I was getting hard thinking what was to come for me in the stairwell.

* * * * *

Today was the day that Chelsea had decided to get even with Chips for the death of her baby father. She figured that today had to be the day because Chips was asking far too many questions. It wasn't that he asked questions that got to her. It was the type of questions that bothered her. Him asking who her child's father was and who she was fucking with after high school unnervered her. If he found that information out he'd fuck her whole plan up. So, before he could ask another question she had to leave his presence. Instead of doing the round that she told Chips she had to do, she went right to her cousin Slump's cell.

Slump was sitting on his bunk smoking some bud when Chelsea showed up. She called him to the door and whispered to him, "Shit gotta go down today cousin. That nigga keep asking questions about my life. If he keep fishing he'll learn that Big Rob is my son's father and my fucking him was a ruse to get him off guard."

"How do you wanna do it? You already know I'm down to buss that nigga head."

"Can you do it during rec?"

"Only if you can set it up so that it's only us two at rec."

"I can do that. Do you have a shank or whatever you guys call it?"

"Nah... You gotta get me one."

"Okay I'll get one. Be ready when you hear your door buzz. Stay in your cell until 5 minutes go by."

"Why wait 5 minutes?"

Nevermind. When your door buzz just go to the stairwell door. He'll be in there unaware of you coming. Hurry up and do the deed and get back to your cell so that you can shower. I'll have a change of clothes and I'll take everything you wear during the situation."

"Cool.. Let me finish this blunt and change. It's a go."

CHAPTER 48

I don't know if it was the idea of about to fuck or if I was comfortable with the set-up or if I was just being plain stupid. Whatever the fuck it was, it had me mentally fucked up because once I got into the stairwell I pulled my sweats down and started stroking my dick as I waited for Chelsea. I visualized her walking in and finding me with all this dick in hand and she drops to her knees and began blessing me with that neck.

However, that's not how it exactly went down. I was stroking my dick while waiting for Chelsea. When the door opened, a nigga walked in!! I was literally caught with my pants down. I tried to pull my pants up but wasn't fast enough because the nigga before me held a thick and long icepick which he attacked me with without warning. His attack was vicious but too confident due to my state of undress. I'm not a stabbing type of nigga but I do know that the way he tried me was wrong because I'm still here telling this story.

Anyhow, he attacked with a downward strike being that I was slightly bent over. I dropped to the floor and rolled back to my feet. When I dropped I had my palms holding onto my sweats. The movements allowed me to have my pants back up when I stood erect again. My boxers weren't on correct but it was adjusted enough for me to defend myself. He tried the same strike motion but I put up my arm and his arm hit mine.

Mind you, I don't leave off my block without my ox. I couldn't spit it out right away so I ran down a flight of stairs and then spit

Within A Week

it into my hand. As soon as my razor hit my hand he landed on the staircase before me. His two efforts at the downward strike were unsuccessful so he tried a side swing. He connected with that. I got hit hard right in my side. At the same time he was swinging I was swinging and my razor struck gold!! He screamed out and released his grip on the icepick. It fell from my side to the floor. He turned and tried to run. I became the predator then. I picked up the icepick and gave chase. He was banging on the door with one hand while the other hand was cupped to his face where my ox chopped him. I've heard that some people go into shock when they're cut in the face. I'm guessing this was one of those times because he was oblivious to me standing behind him as he beat the door. I was in so much pain from the stab but I was carried on by a animal instinct and rage to kill this nigga for even trying me.

My face became tight as I expertly plunged the icepick into his neck. He dropped to the floor and all I heard was gurgling. I jumped onto him and stabbed him repeatedly with the icepick until I passed out from my own blood loss.

Later I learned that I was in critical condition and on life support. With me having the strong will to live, I overcame that shit and recovered. The icepick that I got hit with and used on him was old and rusted. That nasty muthafucka had pierced my lungs and did damage but the doctors cleared me of dying.

After a week in ICU I was given a clean bill of health and normal recovery status; which was bullshit because I kept on drifting in and out of consciousness. The last thing I remembered was my Angel, Nurse Nekesha telling me to stay strong because we're very close to a better place....

EPILOGUE

Chelsea had been reprimanded for allowing Chips and Slump out in stairwell together without an officer present. She has been suspended and she'll possibly be fired when the Feds do their thorough investigation. The knowledge of what's to come has left a sick and scared feeling in her stomach. She knew that once they did their investigation it may come out that she's behind the whole set-up of trying to have Chips killed. She feared that they'll learn of Slump being her family member and of the icepick being removed from the locked and secure safe room within the facility. To top it all off, she knew they'd find out that her son's father was one of Chips victims during his murder spree. She had a lot to be scared of. To only make matters worse, she was pregnant with Chips only child!! In school she often fantasized about having Chip's baby and now she is!!

Part of her felt bad because she really had grown to love Chips and her last knowledge of him was that he was in critical condition. She desperately wanted to see him again. She wasn't sure if she really wanted to see him alive or dead. With him alive he may tell of their fucking. The Feds may order a DNA testing on her pregnancy and easily learn that it's Chip's child.

Chelsea was broken from her thoughts by a loud and insistent pounding on the door. She was rattled by the pounding because she wasn't expecting anyone. She fearfully got off the sofa to answer the door. She looked out the window and saw six or seven unmarked government official vehicles scattered in front. Her heart dropped to her stomach because she just knew that they were there to arrest her. She figured that they figured everything out and her time has come to an end. She wasn't good with acting but she tried her best when she opened the door. The first Agent she saw upon opening the door was none other than Agent Licass. The very same Agent who interviewed her on the day Big Rob was murdered. The very same Agent who pursued Chips with unrelentless measures. Her alarm level increased when he said, "Ms. Jacobs, we have a problem. You need to come with us."

"Come with you? Where? Why?"

"There's some things we need to talk about. Your knowledge and time running the cellblock that housed Mr. Chambers can be very helpful for us. Not only that, you'll be far more safe with us."

"Safe? What do you mean Safe?"

"Mr. Chambers has escaped."

**THE END
OR SO IT SEEM**

Printed in the United States
By Bookmasters